CHRISTMAS IN MY HEART 2

CHRISTMAS IN MY HEART 2

JOE L. WHEELER

REVIEW AND HERALD® PUBLISHING ASSOCIATION
HAGERSTOWN, MD 21740

The author assumes full responsibility for the accuracy of all facts and quotations as cited in this book.

This book was
Edited by Raymond H. Woolsey
Designed by Bill Kirstein
Cover design by Helcio Deslandes
Cover art by Superstock/Currier & Ives
Type set: Goudy Old Style

PRINTED IN U.S.A.

98 97 96 95 94 93   10 9 8 7 6 5 4 3

R&H Cataloging Service
Wheeler, Joe L., 1936–   comp.
    Christmas in my heart.   Book 2.

    1. Christmas stories, American. I. Title:
Christmas in my heart.   Book 2.
          813.010833

ISBN 0-8280-0793-4

Acknowledgments

"Introduction: The 36 Days of Christmas," by Joe L. Wheeler. Copyright 1993. Printed by permission of the author.

"The Littlest Orphan and the Christ Baby," by Margaret Sangster. Included in Sangster's collection, *The Littlest Orphan and Other Christmas Stories*, Round Table Press, New York, 1928.

"The Real Christmas Spirit," by Helen E. Richards. Published in *The Youth's Instructor*, Dec. 25, 1923.

"The Gift of the Magi," by O. Henry (William Sidney Porter). Included in O. Henry's collection, *The Four Million*, Doubleday and Company, New York, 1906.

"Running Away From Christmas," by Annie Hamilton Donnell. Published in *The Youth's Instructor*, Dec. 26, 1916.

"The Last Straw," by Paula McDonald Palangi. Published as a separate book by David C. Cook, Elgin, Illinois, 1992. Reprinted by permission of David C. Cook.

"Have You Seen the Star?" by Margaret Slattery. If anyone can provide knowledge of the origin of this old story, please relay information to Joe L. Wheeler, care of Review and Herald Publishing Association.

"Christmas Island," by Mary Ellen Holmes. Originally published in *The War Cry*. Reprinted by permission of The Salvation Army and *The War Cry*.

"The Tallest Angel." Author and original source unknown. If anyone can provide knowledge of origins of this old story, please relay information to Joe L. Wheeler, care of Review and Herald Publishing Association.

"The Tiny Foot," by Frederic Loomis. Story is included in Loomis's book, *Consultation Room*, Alfred Kuopf, New York, 1939. If anyone can provide knowledge of the whereabouts of surviving Loomis family, please relay such information to Joe L. Wheeler, care of Review and Herald Publishing Association.

"Delayed Delivery," by Cathy Miller. Published in *Northern Life*, Dec. 26, 1992, Sudbury, Ontario, Canada. Printed by permission of the author.

"The Locking in of Lisabeth," by Temple Bailey. If anyone can provide knowledge of earliest publication and date of this old story, please relay this information to Joe L. Wheeler, care of Review and Herald Publishing Association.

"Christmas Magic." Author and original source unknown. If anyone can provide knowledge of the origin of this old story, please relay this information to Joe L. Wheeler, care of Review and Herald Publishing Association.

"A Father for Christmas," Author and original source unknown. If anyone can provide knowledge of the origin of this old story, please relay this information to Joe L. Wheeler, care of Review and Herald Publishing Association.

Contents

Christmas joy is in my heart

The 36 Days of Christmas

Joe L. Wheeler

If we are ever to discover Christmas as the early Christian church knew it, major changes in Christmas observance will need to take place. Instead of our current 24 feverish hours of excess and gift bombardment, we should slow our pace and take time to remember our Lord, to pattern our behavior on Him, the greatest prototype of selfless giving and service for others that the world has ever known.

Merchants won't be happy with us for making such a change, for today Christmas has degenerated to mere sales statistics: "Hurry! There are only x number of shopping days until Christmas."

We will begin each season, as did the Early Church, with the season of the Advent. Around the first of December, we will turn off the television set and leave it off for 36 days. In the place of television we will set up as the focal center of our lives a manger scene, or crèche. We will post an Advent calendar and plan activities for our family that will reflect the spiritual dimensions of the season. Instead of watching beer commercials that shamelessly trade on Christ's birth, death, and resurrection, we will take the family to attend sacred concerts, oratorios, and pageants. We will visit and serve those less fortunate than ourselves. Each evening during the 24 days of Advent we will gather around the fireside (if we have one), share Christmas stories, sing and perform Christian music, play parlor games, and fellowship with our extended family.

It will be a time to turn off glaring lights and substitute the serenity of fireside, candle, and kerosene lamps. We will craft gifts rather than merely buy them in a shopping mall.

When Christmas Eve arrives, and the bells of midnight are followed by Christmas morning, there will yet remain the "Twelve Days of Christmas," culminating with the Day of the Magi (also known as the Epiphany) on January 6.

As was true with the Early Church, the emphasis during the Advent will be on Christ's birth in the flesh, in Bethlehem, the miracle of incarnation. But also important are the concluding 12 days. To early Christians, these represent the days that led up to Christ's second birth, His baptism in the Jordan River. It was then that the Holy Spirit descended upon Him as a dove and, with the Father, testified publicly that the divine circle of three was united for the awesome task ahead.

9

In much of the Christian world today, on each of these 12 days gifts are given. Often, children are given one gift a day, and in turn may give gifts themselves. On January 6, more than one gift is given.

For us and our families, these days can be joyous ones. Note this serendipity: New Year's Day divides the 12 days in half. On this day the family can take time to give thanks, take stock of the past year and the many blessings it has brought, make New Year's resolutions, and look forward to the year to come.

On the seventh day of January, we will tenderly pack up the nativity figures and make plans for the next season.

If we are to be successful in reclaiming Christmas from the amoral media, we shall have to fill the time once wasted on television with something more profitable, something more in tune with the divine. We shall need to develop new traditions.

Las Posadas

Perhaps one of the reasons I still have a childlike love for Christmas is that I was lucky enough to be brought up in two distinctly different cultures: North America and Latin America. I was barely 9 when our family left California for Panama (and then Costa Rica, Guatemala, Dominican Republic, and Mexico). In our home, we waited out that interminable period of time between November 30 and Christmas Eve. But finally it would come. Mother would read us Christmas stories, we would think about the birth of our Lord, we would open the gifts under the pine

Christmas tree—and within hours it would all be over for another year.

Not so with my Latino playmates. For them, the season began during the last days of November, and the enthusiasm and excitement built steadily. In each home would be a crèche, and colorful flowers filled the houses. I was jealous of my friends, so my folks gladly let me purchase nativity figures and arrange my own crèche each year.

Children are loved everywhere, but nowhere, it seems to me, more than "south of the border." (I'll never forget the first time I awoke at 5:00 on the morning of my birthday, to the haunting chords of "Las Mañanitas." My adult friends loved me enough to crawl out of bed in the dead of night, dress, gather with other friends and relatives, tune the guitar, walk to our house, position themselves outside my window, and sing to me. *Me*—just a child!)

To me, the loveliest of Christmas traditions is Las Posadas, which originated in Mexico. Starting near the first of December, children's thoughts center increasingly on the coming nine nights. Who will get to be the Virgin Mary? Who will get to be Joseph? Who will get to turn them away from the door when they knock, seeking "posada" (a place to rest for the night), and who will at last get to welcome them in? Every time the children pass their crèche their thoughts turn to that dramatic reenactment only days away.

Finally, on the night of December 16, nine families choreograph the festivities. The starring roles are assigned to children.

No one who has ever seen "Las Posadas" can possibly forget how moving it is. Once it begins, all else in the life of the town seems to stop while the 2,000-year-old drama is once again played out.

The long journey from Nazareth to Bethlehem is represented by two children. Carrying his staff, "Joseph" leads a donkey. On the donkey's plump back is the most precious thing in the universe, little "Mary," who, we "know," carries within her the Saviour of the world.

Friends and relatives surround the pair as they make their way down the street. These friends also are attired in costumes of the time. The mood is set by candlelight and sacred music. Joseph and Mary and their attendants stop at nine houses. At each door Joseph pleads for "posada"; at each door he is unceremoniously turned away. Except at the ninth house—the door is opened wide, the procession comes in, and all sing their thanks.

For nine consecutive nights the pageant is repeated. But each time it is different, for on each night "posada" is offered at a different home.

The last "posada" I experienced was in Taxco, Mexico, on *La Noche Buena* (Christmas Eve). Even now, a quarter of a century later, I can still envision that moment when the procession was welcomed into the inn where my family and I were staying: the sweet, high sounds of the children's voices as they sang, and above all, the boy who, for the moment,

was Joseph, and the girl who *was* Mary.

When I compare that feeling of reverence and awe to Christmas in America, I could cry. On that holiest of nights, "La Noche Buena," all over America children are ripping paper off gaily-wrapped packages, scanning the contents, and feverishly grabbing the next. But in much of the Christian world children are preparing to go with their parents to the cathedral, church, or chapel, there to see the nativity scene; there to hear the Christmas music, the mighty organ, and the midnight bells welcoming the birth of the Christ-child.

The next morning is a joyful one for those children, but not because of avalanches of presents, although there may be a few. There is no Santa Claus for, after all, this is the Lord's birth being celebrated. There are yet 12 more wonderful Christmas days before that most anticipated day, January 6.

I can still remember how excited my friends next door were as they eagerly waited for the religious processions of the Three Kings, and the gifts the kings would leave for them during the night. The Magi. Not Santa Claus.

It's not that I am against Santa Claus, for he represents another special part of my Christmas memories: I can hear my red-and-white-suited Santa of a father playing Christmas carols on his harmonica as he draws near the front door. But I am revolted that the memory of a wonderful and generous Christian gentleman, St. Nicholas, has been perverted to the pandering of seasonal merchandise to avaricious children, vigorously

11

encouraged to greed beyond belief by the advertising media and those who buy their services.

Is it strange that I long for the 36 Days of Christmas as they are enjoyed south of the border?

The Second Collection

It has been an incredible 18 months. All of us involved in the production of *Christmas in My Heart* had high hopes for the volume, but the reality has turned out to be beyond all our projections. We knew that *we* loved the stories and the format, but would *others*? We did not have long to wait: there was a short time lag of about three to four weeks while the initial copies were being scrutinized; then they began moving all over the country. By December, I had appointments for book signings every couple days. In one five-hour period I inscribed more than 600 books. It became common to see people purchasing 10, 20, 30 or more copies at a time.

And the mail! It started early and has kept coming to this very day. Not one negative note that I can remember—that's the wonder. Clearly, the stories have touched hearts in a way that only such stories can. Looking back, we can see how the Lord was with us each step of the way. One individual, who had read straight through the book over a 24-hour-period, told me that reaching the last line of "Meditation" was like "an altar call to the whole book."

It has been gathered to the hearts of all generations, from the youngest to the oldest; from deeply committed Christians to those who have lost their way and are seeking for a viable philosophy of life; from families who cement their bonds by sharing the stories to divorcées who read the stories as therapy.

The never-ceasing waves of mail (averaging up to five letters a day) represent a new dimension in my life, and has brought home the realization that out of my all-too-frail efforts the Lord has created a ministry. I am awed by His incredible choreography.

Over and over again, the letter writers urge us to keep the stories coming. And just to make sure, they send me new ones, recent ones, well-loved ones, and old ones. The result is that from once wondering whether we could maintain the story quality level in future books we now are reduced to tears by the wonderful ones we leave out.

Because of high sales and this avalanche of responses, I was given the green light to rush this second collection to publication.

You voted a number of these stories in, by special request: "The Gift of the Magi," "The Littlest Orphan," "The Locking in of Lisabeth," "The Tiny Foot," "Have You Seen the Star?"; and "Delayed Delivery."

I have taken occasional editorial liberties, updating words or terms that have become archaic or have acquired negative connotations.

Coda

I look forward to hearing from you, and *do* keep the stories coming! You may reach me by writing to:
Joe L. Wheeler, Ph.D.
c/o Review and Herald Pub. Assn.
55 West Oak Ridge Drive
Hagerstown, MD 21740

The Littlest Orphan and the Christ Baby

Margaret E. Sangster

This particular story has been around for many years; nevertheless, it is just as beautiful and timely as it ever was. We are supposedly less sentimental today than we were when it was written, but maybe we were better off when we weren't ashamed to cry.

My beloved mother read it to us many times when I was growing up, and for this second collection she had but one request: "Please include 'The Littlest Orphan.' "

As I researched at the Library of Congress, in a very old collection I discovered the original text of the story, significantly different from the eroded version I had always known—and more beautiful.

Margaret Sangster is little known today, but early in this century she was one of the most loved and appreciated writers and editors of inspirational literature in America.

The Littlest Orphan gazed up into the face of the Christ Baby, who hung gilt-framed and smiling above the mantel-shelf. The mantel was dark, made of a black, mottled marble that suggested tombstones, and the long room, despite its rows of neat, white beds, gave an impression of darkness, too. But the picture above the mantel sparkled and scintillated and threw off an aura of sheer happiness. Even the neat "In Memoriam" card tacked to the wall directly under it could not detract from its joy. All of rosy babyhood, all of unspoiled laughter, all of the beginnings of life were in that picture! And the Littlest Orphan sensed it, even though he did not quite understand.

The Matron was coming down the room with many wreaths, perhaps a dozen of them, braceleting her thin arm. The wreaths were just a trifle dusty, their imitation holly leaves spoke plaintively of successive years of hard usage. But it was only two days before Christmas and the wreaths would not show up so badly under artificial light. The board of trustees, coming for the entertainment on Christmas Eve, never arrived until the early winter dusk had settled down. And the wreaths could be laid away, as soon as the holiday was past, for another 12 months.

The Littlest Orphan, staring up at the picture, did not hear the Matron's approaching footsteps. True, the Matron wore rubber heels—but any other orphan in the whole asylum would have heard her. Only the Littlest Orphan, with his thin, sensitive face and his curious fits of absorption, could have ignored her coming. He started painfully as her sharp voice cut into the silence.

"John," she said, and the frost that made such pretty lacework upon the window pane wrought havoc with her voice: *"John, what are you doing here?"*

The Littlest Orphan answered after the manner of all small boy-children. "Nothin'!" he said.

Standing before him, the Matron—who was a large woman—seemed to tower. "You are not telling the truth, John," she said. "You have no right to be in the dormitory at this hour. Report to Miss Mace at once" (Miss Mace was the primary teacher) "and tell her that I said you were to write five pages in your copybook. *At once!*"

With hanging head the Littlest Orphan turned away. It seemed terribly unfair, although it was against the rules to spend any but sleeping hours in the dormitory! He was just learning to write, and five pages meant a whole afternoon of cramped fingers and tired eyes. But how could he explain to this grim woman that the Christ Baby fascinated him, charmed him, and comforted him? How could he explain that the Christ Baby's wide eyes had a way of glancing down, almost with understanding, into his own? How could he tell, with the few weak words of his vocabulary, that he loved the Christ Baby, whose smile was so tenderly sweet? That he spent much of

his time standing, as he stood now, in the shadow of that smile? He trudged away with never a word, down the length of the room, his clumsy shoes making a feeble clatter on the bare boards of the floor. When he was almost at the door, the Matron called after him.

"Don't drag your feet, John!" she commanded. And so he walked the rest of the way on tiptoe. And closed the door very softly after him.

The halls had already been decorated with long streamers of red and green crepe paper that looped along, in a half-hearted fashion, from picture to picture. The stair railing was wound with more of the paper, and the schoolroom, where Miss Mace sat stiffly behind a broad desk, was vaguely brightened by red cloth poinsettias set here and there at random. But the color of them was not reflected in the Littlest Orphan's heart, as he delivered his message and received in return a battered copybook.

As he sat at his desk, and writing laboriously about the cat who ate the rat and the dog who ran after the cat, he could hear the other orphans playing outside in the courtyard. Always they played from four o'clock, when school was over, until five-thirty, which was suppertime. It was a rule to play from four to five-thirty. They were running and shouting together, but in a stilted way.

The Littlest Orphan did not envy them much. They were all older and stronger than he, and their games were sometimes hard to enjoy. He had been the last baby taken before a new ruling, making 6 years the minimum entrance age, had gone through. And he was only 5 years old now. Perhaps it was his very littleness that made the Matron more intolerant of him—he presented to her a problem that could not be met in a mass way. His clothing had to be several sizes smaller than the other clothing; his lessons less advanced. And so on.

Drearily he wrote. And listened, between sentences, to the scratching pen of Miss Mace . . . The dog had caught the cat. And now the man beat the dog. And then it was time to start all over again, back at the place where the cat ate the rat. Two pages, three pages, four pages . . . Surreptitiously the Littlest Orphan moved his fingers, one by one, and wondered that he was still able to move them. Then, working slowly, he finished the last page and handed the copybook back to the teacher. As she studied it, her face softened slightly.

"Why did the Matron punish you, John?" she asked, as if on impulse, as she made a correction in a sentence.

The Littlest Orphan hesitated for a second. And then: "I shouldn't have been in the dormitory," he said slowly. "An' I was!"

Again Miss Mace asked a question.

"But what," she queried, "were you doing there? Why weren't you out playing with the other children?"

She didn't comment upon the fault, but the Littlest Orphan knew that she, also, thought the pun-ishment rather severe. Only it isn't policy to criticize a superior's method of discipline. He answered her second question gravely.

"I was lookin' at th' Christ Baby over the mantel," he said.

As if to herself, Miss Mace spoke. "You mean the picture Mrs. Benchly gave in memory of her son," she murmured, "the pastel." And then, "Why were you looking at it—" She hesitated, and the Littlest Orphan didn't know that she had almost said "dear."

Shyly the child spoke, and wistfulness lay across his thin, small face—an unrealized wistfulness. "He looks so—nice—" said the Littlest Orphan gently, "like he had a mother, maybe."

* * * * *

Supper that night was brief, and after supper there were carols to practice in the assembly room. The Littlest Orphan, seated at the extreme end of the line, enjoyed the singing. The red-headed boy, who fought so often in the courtyard, had a high, thrilling soprano. Listening to him as he sang the solo parts made the Littlest Orphan forget a certain black eye, and a nose that had once been swollen and bleeding. Made him forget lonely hours when he had lain uncomforted in his bed, as a punishment for quarreling.

The red-headed boy was singing something about "gold and frank-kin-sense, and myrrh." The Littlest Orphan told himself that they must be very beautiful things. Gold—the Christ Baby's frame was of gold, but frank-kin-sense and myrrh were unguessed

15

names. Maybe they were flowers, real flowers that smelled pretty, not red cloth ones. He shut his eyes, singing automatically, and imagined what these flowers looked like—the color and shape of their petals, and whether they grew on tall lily stalks or on short pansy stems. And then the singing was over and he opened his eyes with a start and realized that the Matron was speaking.

"Before you go to bed," she was saying, "I want you to understand that you must be on your good behavior until after the trustees leave tomorrow evening. You must not make any disorder in the corridors or in the dormitories—they have been especially cleaned and dusted. You must pay strict attention to the singing; the trustees like to hear you sing! They will all be here, even Mrs. Benchly, who has not visited us since her son died. And if one of you misbehaves—"

She stopped abruptly, but her silence was crowded with meaning, and many a child squirmed uncomfortably in his place. It was only after a moment that she spoke again.

"Good night!" she said abruptly.

And the orphans chorused back, "Good night."

* * * * *

Undressing carefully and swiftly, for the dormitory was cold and the gas lights were dim, the Littlest Orphan wondered about the trustees—and in particular about the Mrs. Benchly who had lost her son. All trustees were ogres to asylum children, but the Littlest Orphan couldn't help feeling that Mrs. Benchly was the least ogre-like of them all. Somehow she was a part of the Christ Baby's picture, and it was a part of her. If she were responsible for it, she could not be all bad! So ruminating, the Littlest Orphan said his brief prayers—any child who forgot his prayers was punished severely—and slid between the sheets into his bed.

Some orphans made a big lump under their bed covers. The red-headed boy was stocky, and so were others. Some of them were almost fat. But the Littlest Orphan made hardly any lump at all. The sheet, the cotton blanket, and the spread went over him with scarcely a ripple. Often the Littlest Orphan had wished that there might be another small boy who could share his bed—he took up such a tiny section of it. Another small boy would have made the bed seem warmer, somehow, and less lonely. Once two orphans had come to the asylum, and they were brothers. They had shared things—beds and desks and books. Maybe brothers were unusual gifts from a surprisingly blind providence, gifts that were granted only once in a hundred years! More rare, even, than mothers.

Mothers—the sound of the word had a strange effect upon the Littlest Orphan, even when he said it silently in his soul. It meant so much that he did not comprehend, so much for which he vaguely hungered. Mothers stood for warm arms, and kisses, and soft words. Mothers meant punishments, too, but gentle punishment that did not really come from away inside.

Often the Littlest Orphan had heard the rest talking stealthily about mothers. Some of them could actually remember having owned one! But the Littlest Orphan could not remember. He had arrived at the asylum as a baby, delicate and frail and too young for memories that would later come to bless him and to cause a strange, sharp sort of hurt. When the rest spoke of bedtime stories, and lullabies, and sugar cookies, he listened, wide-eyed and half-incredulous, to their halting sentences.

It was growing very cold in the dormitory, and it was dark. Even the faint flicker of light had been taken away. The Littlest Orphan wiggled his toes under the bottom blanket, and wished that sleep would come. Some nights it came quickly, but this night—perhaps he was overtired, and it was so cold!

As a matter of habit his eyes searched through the dark for the place where the Christ Baby hung. He could not distinguish even the dim outlines of the gilt frame, but he knew that the Christ Baby was rosy and chubby and smiling, that his eyes were deeply blue and filled with cheer. Involuntarily the Littlest Orphan stretched out his thin hands and dropped them back again against the spread. All about him the darkness lay like a smothering coat, and the Christ Baby, even though He smiled, was invisible. The other children were sleeping. All up and down the long room sounded their regular breathing, but the Littlest Orphan could not sleep. He wanted some-

thing that he was unable to define, wanted it with such a burning intensity that the tears crowded into his eyes. He sat up abruptly in his bed, a small, shivering figure with quivering lips and a baby ache in his soul that had never really known babyhood.

Loneliness—it swept about him. More disheartening than the cold. More enveloping than the darkness. There was no fear in him of the shadows in the corner, of the creaking shutters and the narrow stair. Such fears are discouraged early in children who live by rule and routine. No, it was a feeling more poignant than fear, a feeling that clutched at him and squeezed his small body until it was dry and shaking and void of expression.

Of all the sleeping dormitory full of children, the Littlest Orphan was the only child who knew the ache of such loneliness. Even the ones who had been torn away from family ties had, each one of them, something beautiful to keep preciously close. But the Littlest Orphan had nothing—nothing . . . The loneliness filled him with a strange impulse, an impulse that sent him sliding over the edge of his bed with small arms outflung.

All at once he was crossing the floor on bare, mouse-quiet feet, past the placidly sleeping children, past the row of lockers, past the table with its neat cloth and black-bound, impressive guest-book. Past everything until he stood, a white spot in the blackness, directly under the mantel. The Christ Baby hung above him. And, though the Littlest Orphan could not see, he felt that the blue eyes were looking down tenderly. All at once he wanted to touch the Christ Baby, to hold him tight, to feel the sweetness and warmth of Him. Tensely, still moved by the curious impulse, he tiptoed back to where the table stood. Carefully he laid the guest book on the floor; carefully he removed the white cloth. And then staggering under the, to him, great weight, he carried the table noiselessly back with him. Though it was really a small light table, the Littlest Orphan breathed hard as he set it down. He had to rest, panting, for a moment, before he could climb up on it.

All over the room lay silence, broken only by the sleepy sounds of the children. The Littlest Orphan listened almost prayerfully as he clambered upon the table top and drew himself to an erect position. His small hands groped along the mantel shelf, touched the lower edge of the gilt frame. But the Christ Baby was still out of reach.

Feverishly, obsessed with one idea, the Littlest Orphan raised himself on tiptoe. His hands gripped the chill marble of the mantel. Tugging, twisting— all with the utmost quiet—he pulled himself up until he was kneeling upon the mantel shelf. Quivering with nervousness as well as the now intense cold, he finally stood erect. And then, only then, was he able to feel the wire and nail that held the Christ Baby's frame against the wall. His numb fingers loosened the wire carefully. And then at last the picture was in his arms.

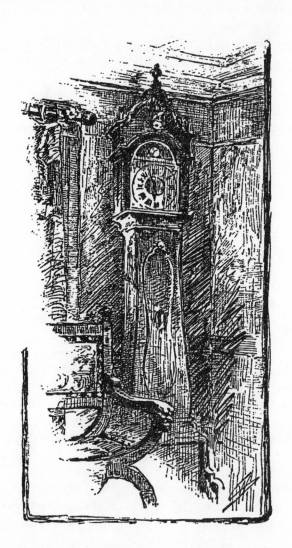

It was heavy, the picture. And hard. Not soft and warm as he had somehow expected it to be. But it was the Christ Baby, nevertheless. Holding it close, the Littlest Orphan fell to speculating upon the ways of getting down, now that both of his hands were occupied. It would be hard to slide from the mantel to the table, and from table to floor, with neither sound nor mishap.

His eyes troubled, his mouth a wavering line in his pinched face, the Littlest Orphan crowded back against the wall. The darkness held now the vague menace of depth. Destruction lurked in a single mis-step. It had been a long way up. It would be even longer going down. And he had the Christ Baby, as well as himself, to care for.

Gingerly he advanced one foot over the edge of the mantel—and drew it back. Sharply. He almost screamed in sudden terror. It was as if the dark had reached out long, bony fingers to pull him from his place of safety. He wanted to raise his hands to his face, but he could not release his hold upon the gilt frame. All at once he realized that his hands were growing numb with the cold and that his feet were numb, too.

The minutes dragged by. Somewhere a clock struck, many times. The Littlest Orphan had never heard the clock strike so many times, at night, before. He cowered back until it seemed to his scared, small mind that he would sink into the wall. And then, as the clock ceased striking, he heard another sound—a sound that brought dread to his heart. It was a step in the hall, a heavy, firm step that, despite rubber heels, was now clearly recognizable. It would be the Matron, making her rounds of the building before she went to bed. As the steps came nearer along the hall, a light, soft and yellow, seemed to glow in the place. It would be the lamp that she carried in her hand.

The Matron reached the door—peered in. And then, with lamp held high, she entered the room. Her swift glance swept the row of white beds—each, but one, with its sleeping occupant.

The Littlest Orphan, on the mantel, clutched the Christ Baby closer in his arms. And waited. It seemed to him that his shivering must shake the room. He gritted his teeth convulsively, as the Matron's eyes found his tumbled, empty bed.

Hastily, forgetting to be quiet, the woman crossed the room. She pulled back the spread, the blanket. And then, as if drawn by a magnet, her eyes lifted, traveled across the room. And found the small, white figure that pressed back into the narrow space. Her voice was sharper even than her eyes when she spoke.

"John," she called abruptly, and her anger made her forget to be quiet. *"What are you doing up there?"*

Across the top of the Christ Baby's gilt frame, the eyes of the Littlest Orphan stared into the eyes of the Matron with something of the fascination that one sees in the eyes of a bird charmed by a cat or a snake. In narrow, white beds, all over the room, children were stirring, pulling themselves erect, staring. One child snickered behind a sheltering hand. But the

Littlest Orphan was conscious only of the Matron. He waited for her to speak again. In a moment she did.

"John," she said, and her voice was burning, and yet chill, with rage, "you are a bad boy. *Come down at once!"*

His eyes blank with sheer fright, his arms clasping the picture close, the Littlest Orphan answered the tone of that voice. With quivering lips he advanced one foot, then the other. And stepped into the space that was the room below. He was conscious that some child screamed—he himself did not utter a sound. And that the Matron started forward. And then he struck the table and rolled with it, and the Christ Baby's splintering picture, into the darkness.

* * * * *

The Littlest Orphan spent the next day in bed, with an aching head and a wounded heart. The pain of his bruises did not make a great difference; neither did the threats of the Matron penetrate his consciousness. Only the bare space over the mantel mattered—only the blur of blue and yellow and red upon the hearth, where the pastel had struck. Only the knowledge that the Christ Baby, the meaning of all light and happiness, was no more, troubled him.

There was a pleasant stir about the asylum. An excited child, creeping into the dormitory, told the Littlest Orphan that one of the trustees had sent a tree. And that another was donating ice cream. And that there were going to be presents. But the Littlest

Orphan did not even smile. His wan face was set and drawn. Dire punishment waited him after his hurts were healed. And there would be no Christ Baby to go to for comfort and cheer when the punishment was over.

The morning dragged on. Miss Mace brought his luncheon of bread and milk and was as kind to him as she dared to be—your Miss Maces have been made timorous by a too forceful world. Once, during the early afternoon, the Matron came in to examine his bruised head, and once a maid came to rub the colored stains from the hearth. The Littlest Orphan caught his breath as he watched her.

And then it began to grow dark, and the children were brought upstairs to be washed and dressed in clean blouses for the entertainment. They had been warned not to talk with him, and they obeyed—for there were folk watching and listening. But even so, flickers of conversation—excited, small-boy conversation—drifted to the Littlest Orphan's waiting ears.

Someone had said there was to be a Santa Claus. In a red suit and a white beard. Perhaps . . . it was true. The Littlest Orphan slid down under the covers and pulled the sheet high over his aching head. He didn't want the rest to know that he was crying.

The face-washing was accomplished swiftly. Just as swiftly were the blouses adjusted to the last tie, string, and button. And then the children filed downstairs, and the Littlest Orphan was left alone again. He pulled himself up gingerly until he sat

20

erect, and buried his face in his hands.

Suddenly, from downstairs, came the sound of music. First, the tiny piano, and then the voices of the children as they sang. Automatically the Littlest Orphan joined in, his voice quavering weakly through the empty place. He didn't want to sing— there was neither rhythm nor melody in his heart. But he had been taught to sing those songs, and sing them he must.

First, there was "O Little Town of Bethlehem." And then a carol. And then the one about "Gold and frank-kin-sense and myrrh." Strange that the words did not mean flowers tonight! And then there was a hush—perhaps it was a prayer. And then a burst of clapping and a jumble of glad cries. Perhaps that was the Santa Claus in his trappings of white and scarlet. The Littlest Orphan's tears came like hot rain to his tired eyes.

There was a sound in the hall. A rubber-heeled step on the bare floor. The Littlest Orphan slid down again under the covers, until only the bandage on the brow was at all visible. When the Matron stooped over him, she could not even glimpse his eyes. With a vigorous hand she jerked aside the covers.

"Sick or not," she told him, "You've got to come downstairs. Mrs. Benchly wants to see the boy who broke her son's memorial picture. I'll help you with your clothes."

Trembling violently, the Littlest Orphan allowed himself to be wedged into undies and a blouse and a pair of coarse, dark trousers. He laced his shoes with fingers that shook with mingled fear and weakness. And then he followed the Matron out of the dormitory and through the long halls, with their mocking festoons of red and green crepe paper, and into the assembly room where the lights were blinding and the Christmas tree was a blaze of glory.

The trustees sat at one end of the room, the far end. There was a mass of dark colors, blacks and browns and somber grays. Following in the wake of the Matron, the Littlest Orphan stumbled toward them. Mrs. Benchly—would she beat him in front of all the rest? Would she leap at him accusingly from that dark mass? He felt smaller than he had ever felt before, and more inadequate.

The children were beginning to sing again. But despite their singing, the Matron spoke. Not loudly, as she did to the children, but with a curious deference.

"This is John, Mrs. Benchly," she said, "the child who broke the picture."

Biting his lips, so that he would not cry out, the Littlest Orphan stood in the vast shadow of the Matron. He shut his eyes. Perhaps if this Mrs. Benchly meant to strike him, it would be best to have his eyes shut. And then suddenly a voice came, a voice so soft that somehow he could almost feel the velvet texture of it.

"Poor child," said the voice. "He's frightened. And ill, too. Come here, John. I won't hurt you, dear."

Opening his eyes incredulously, the Littlest Orphan stared past the Matron into the sort of face small children dream about. Violet-eyed and tender. Lined, perhaps, and sad about the mouth, and wistful. But so sweet! Graying hair, with a bit of wave in it, brushed back from a broad, white brow. And slim, white, reaching hands. The Littlest Orphan went forward without hesitation. Something about this lady was reminiscent of the Christ Baby. As her white hand touched his, tightened on it, he looked up into her face with the ghost of a smile.

The children had crowded almost informally to the other end of the room, toward the tree. The dark mass of the trustees was dissolving, breaking up into fragments, that followed the children. One of the trustees laughed aloud. Not at all like an ogre. A sudden sense of gladness began, for no understandable reason, to steal across the Littlest Orphan's consciousness. Rudely the voice of the Matron broke in upon it.

"I have warned the children," she said, "not to disturb anything. Last evening, before they retired, John deliberately disobeyed. And the picture is ruined in consequence. What do you think we had better do about it, Mrs. Benchly?"

For a moment the lady with the dream face did not speak. She was drawing the Littlest Orphan nearer, until he touched the satin folds of her black gown, and despite the Matron's voice, he was not afraid. When at last she answered the Matron, he did not flinch.

"I think," she said gently, "that I'll ask you to leave us. I would like to talk with John—alone."

As the Matron walked stiffly away, down the length of the room, Mrs. Benchly lifted the Littlest Orphan unto her lap.

"I know," she said, and her voice was even gentler than it had been, "that you didn't mean to break the picture. Did you, dear?"

Eagerly the Littlest Orphan answered, "Oh, no—ma'am!" he told her. "I didn't mean t' break th' Christ Baby."

The woman's arms were about him. They tightened suddenly. "You're so young," she said; "you're such a mite of a thing. I doubt if you could understand why I had the picture made, why I gave it to the home here, to be hung in the dormitory. My little son was all I had after my husband died. And his nursery—it was such a pretty room—had a Christ Child picture on the wall. And my boy always loved the picture . . . And so when he—left—" Her voice faltered. "I had an artist copy it. I—I couldn't part with the original! And I sent it to a place where there would be many small boys, who could enjoy it as my son had always—" Her voice broke.

The Littlest Orphan stared in surprise at the lady's face. Her violet eyes were misted like April blossoms with the dew upon them. Her lips quivered. Could it be that she, too, was lonesome and afraid? His hand crept up until it touched her soft cheek.

"I *loved* th' Christ Baby," he said simply.

The lady looked at him. With an effort she

downed the quaver in her voice. "I can't believe," she said at last, "that you destroyed the picture purposely. No matter what she"—her glance rested upon the Matron's stiff figure, half a room away—"may think! John, dear, did you mean to spoil the gift I gave—in my small boy's name? Oh, I'm sure you didn't."

All day long the Littlest Orphan had lived in fear and agony of soul. All day long he had known pain, physical pain and the pain of suspense. Suddenly he buried his face in the lady's neck—he had never known before that there was a place in ladies' necks just made for tiny heads—and the tears came. Choked by sobs, he spoke.

"No'm," he sobbed, "I didn't mean to . . . It was only because I was cold. And lonesome. And th' bed was—big. An' all th' rest was asleep. An' the Christ Baby always looked so pink . . . an' glad . . . an' warm. An' I wanted t' take him inter my bed an' cuddle close!" He burrowed his head deeper into the neck— "so that I wouldn't be cold anymore. Or lonesome— anymore."

The lady's arms tightened about the Littlest Orphan's body until the pressure almost hurt, but it was a nice sort of hurt. It shocked her, somehow, to feel the thinness of that body. And her tears fell quite unrestrained upon the Littlest Orphan's bandaged head. And then all at once she bent over. And her lips pressed, ever so tenderly, upon the place where his cheek almost met her ear.

"Not to be cold," she whispered, more to herself than to the Littlest Orphan, "or lonesome anymore! To have the nursery opened again—and the sound of the tiny feet in the empty rooms. To have the Christ Child smiling down upon a sleeping little boy. To kiss bruises away again . . . Not to be lonesome anymore, or cold—"

Suddenly she tilted back the Littlest Orphan's head, was looking deep, deep into his bewildered eyes.

"John," she said, and his name sounded so different when she said it, "how would you like to come away from here, and live in my house, with me? How would you like to be my boy?"

A silence had crept over the other end of the room. One of the trustees, who wore a clerical collar, had mounted the platform. He was reading from the Bible that visiting ministers read from of a Sunday. His voice rang, resonant and rich as an organ tone, through the room.

"For unto us a child is born," he read, "*unto us a son is given.*"

The Littlest Orphan, with a sigh of utter happiness, crowded closer into the arms that held him.

And it was Christmas Eve!

The Real Christmas Spirit

Helen E. Richards

Traditions are not necessarily static, unchanging. They can become boring and stuffy. There may come times when a bit of freshness is needed. Improvisation more likely will bring vitality than will Christmas-as-usual.

Well, in the case of the Davenports, Christmas-as-usual was out of the question—so what then?

I n a prosperous Middle Western town, on the east side, at the upper end of a long avenue of comfortable homes, the street veers suddenly to the right and ends in Cedar Hill, a blind but beautiful alley, bordered with lawns, decorated at this time of year with strange, nobby figures of gunny sacking wound with cord and with piles of straw overlaid with boards. Back of these suggestions of the landscape gardener stand four houses, wide-spreading, luxurious—Cedar Hill homes of the Davenports, the Clydes, the Lees, and the Ludingtons.

On Christmas Eve it was the custom for Cordelia Davenport to give a recital, and the Clydes and the Lees and the Ludingtons came laden with their articles of commerce, and hung them on the Davenport Christmas tree at the end of a long drawing room. The little group of families on Cedar Hill always celebrated royally, because it was within the power of Cedar Hill residents to do so.

"And Cedar Hill leads the town," quoted James Davenport, Jr., to his sister.

James, Jr., was taller than his father, and he carried himself with a regal air in spite of his extreme youth. He drew down the library shades and flung himself into an armchair.

"Sis, what do you say to going to Meredith's for programs? They have some gorgeous new leather things. I say white morocco, with the Davenport coat of arms in gold and blue. How does that strike you?"

"And mistletoe instead of holly. Borts are taking orders now," supplemented Sis. "And I want Mother to try that new caterer on West Fifth. They say he is so much better than—" She stopped suddenly and looked up at James with a startled expression. Both listened intently. They heard the voice of their mother talking to James, Sr., in the music room.

"It isn't right, James, with all the financial reverses you have suffered this year and all the calls there are for charity, that we should spend so lavishly.

I shall never forget how nearly we came to losing the old home itself. We ought not to have any recital at all!"

"No recital!" James, Sr., gasped. "What will the Ludingtons say?" he cried.

"The Ludingtons can be thankful that they live in well-favored America, and not in starving Germany."

James, Jr., slipped from his chair and caught his sister's arm.

"What is it?" he whispered. "What are they talking about?"

"Hush!"

James, Sr., was speaking again. "We can manage the recital, I think, Cordelia, and have something to give besides," he said in a low, generous voice.

"Then we ought to give twice as much, and go without the recital," insisted Mrs. Davenport. "It would be positively wicked for us to have the usual orgy of presents and feasting while there is such great need. The Davenports have always led. Let us lead now, in giving—in sacrifice."

"What will the children say?" asked her husband, suddenly.

"Never mind what they say, James. They need just this kind of experience. They are spendthrifts, both of them. Jim, Jr., hasn't the first notion of the value of money, and as for Sis—we've encouraged her in—oh, well, never mind. We always had more than enough, until the stock company failed. Perhaps it hasn't been best not to let them know about our

worries," she added thoughtfully.

Sis gazed at her brother solemnly. "Are we that bad, Jim?" she questioned under her breath."

He was silent. The fire in the grate crackled and snapped and leaped and fell. The voices in the music room had dropped to a lower key.

"What about stock failing?" James, Jr., asked finally. "I heard rumors at college, but I didn't suppose it was really so, when Dad didn't mention anything."

James, Jr., slung himself forward, resting his chin in his hands. Sis watched him in silence.

"We'll let the morocco programs go—eh, Sis?" he laughed shortly. Then he looked up. "See here. How much money have you?"

"Not more than five dollars, I guess. I spent the rest for—"

"And I haven't a cent!"

Sis gazed at him tremulously. "We can't have any Christmas," she faltered.

James, Jr., stood up. In the firelight, against the dark background of the library, he loomed like a young giant, his features standing out white, vivid, forceful, with all the Davenport pride and reserve. Quietly he put his hands in his pockets and stared into the fire.

"We have always led, Sis, as Mother says," he said slowly; "and our house has always been gay at Christmas time. We have to keep it up!"

"But the money, Jim—if we—"

"We can celebrate Christmas without money,

Sis. What's family pride for? It isn't money pride, Sis, it's the real article. We'll have our party just the same. And we'll do it on what money we can scare up between us!"

The time had been, years before, when the Cedar Hill families were poor, when the Davenport Christmas party had been very gay but very economical. But of late years, money and social rivalry had increased the expenditure and stunted the gaiety. Cordelia Davenport had been the leader, and if sometimes she sighed for more sincerity and less show in their social affairs, still it had not occurred to her that the situation could be remedied. So used had she become to professional singers and high-priced caterers that to forego these luxuries, even from a sense of duty, meant no Christmas festivity, and she sighed as she thought how they would miss the annual gathering.

James, Sr., too, much as he hated the stately social functions, began to realize a loss as the holidays approached.

"No Christmas this year," he said with a shrug as he met Mr. Clyde at the corner and they turned toward Cedar Hill for dinner.

"That's all right," declared Clyde, seriously. "We're cutting out some things, too. Rather hard on the children."

Silently the two men strode on up the hill, and it did not occur to either of them that they could celebrate without an outlay.

"What can you do without money?" asked Davenport, gloomily.

"I know," nodded Clyde. "It doesn't rain Christmas doings—you have to buy them."

It was a few days before Christmas, and Cordelia Davenport was making her afternoon toilet before a tall mirror in her dressing room. Tall mirrors were rather a specialty with her, and if any one of her family wished to give her an expensive present, he knew without asking that she could find space somewhere for another mirror—or for a cut-glass candlestick. She was not sure which of these she liked best. James, Jr., once said that his mother ought to live in a glass house.

Today, as Mrs. Davenport dressed, she saw reflected in her mirror the figure of a woman crossing the street and aiming straight for her front door. It was a portly figure, increased to absurdity by a huge collaret and a muff the size of two Angora cats.

"Madam Ludington!" exclaimed Cordelia. "What can she possibly want?"

This question did not imply that Madam's calls were infrequent, but merely that her movements were sometimes social maneuvers. The recent stricture in the Christmas expenditure of the Davenports altered the social opportunities.

"It is so lovely of you to have us just the same as ever," Madam greeted Mrs. Davenport sincerely and cordially, "just lovely! It's the true Christmas spirit. You don't know how we all appreciate it."

Cordelia Davenport smiled vaguely. Was this sarcasm? She remembered uncomfortably the costly present she had received from Madam a year ago.

"Yes?" she parried pleasantly.

"And the invitations are too delightful. So informal. I told Sis I hoped she would always come hereafter to deliver them—she is growing into a very charming young lady."

"Yes," Cordelia assented, "I'm very proud of my girl—she is so trustworthy."

What had Sis done? What had happened? But Sis *was* trustworthy. Mrs. Davenport said it over frantically to herself while she smiled at her guest.

"We are all so delighted with your idea of entertaining us simply. It is so different!"

Madam Ludington's good faith was evident, but Cordelia could scarcely appreciate it—she was too much alarmed.

"I think," she said with sudden inspiration, and she marveled at herself as she said it, "that a merry Christmas is not dependent on a bank account."

The plump, shrewd face of her neighbor lighted suddenly. "But we had forgotten that!" she exclaimed.

When James, Sr., came home for dinner, he was unusually gay. His wife told him of Madam Ludington's visit.

"Trust the Davenports for upholding the family honor," he laughed easily; "they've never failed yet, and they never will. James, Jr., and Sis came into the office this afternoon and told me they were going to entertain the usual crowd on five dollars. What do you think of that? Sis said she would bake four dozen cookies after some recipe she learned at school."

Cordelia stared.

"Four dozen cookies!" she cried. "They aren't expecting to feed Madam Ludington and the rest on *cookies?*"

James, Sr., looked alarmed. This appalling deduction had not occurred to him. But relief at the attitude of his son and daughter had made him feel lighthearted.

"Well, perhaps that isn't enough," he returned quickly; "Madam is a hearty eater." Then they both laughed till they cried.

"It will be perfectly awful," she sobbed, "to give those people cookies, but the children mean well!"

Then she dried her eyes and went to arrange her hair. But she stopped short in astonishment.

"James!" she called. "James, come here!"

Before them, where the long broad mirror had hung, was a plain bare wall, and near the center, in an inadequate attempt to fill the space, hung James, Sr.'s, shaving glass. Stuck to the wall with a pin was a bit of paper scrawled in the handwriting of Jim, Jr. "Merry Christmas, folks!" it challenged. They were disarmed. There was nothing to do but laugh and wonder. The little paper as much as said: "Don't ask any questions."

James, Sr., was silent for a space.

"Cordelia," he said finally, "we've grown away—far away from the old simple good times. Perhaps the children can bring us back. Let's not worry about their plans. We can trust them. Let's be game."

Mrs. Davenport gazed at him contemplatively, a

slight smile beginning to curl about the corners of her mouth.

"Why—" she hesitated, "why—perhaps you're right."

That night, when James, Sr., came downstairs to dinner, he tripped on an innocent-looking yellow bag that stood on the lower step. By an agile leap he saved his life and landed on the rug, while a little stream of lemons rolled gaily across the polished floor.

"There!" muttered Jim, Jr., to Sis in the dining room. "I forgot to take away that bag."

A new faction had arisen at Cedar Hill, eager, inventive, at work for the preservation of a nearly lost holiday. All that Merry Christmas had meant, all that it had failed to mean because of worldliness and social bickerings, hovered fantastically before the residents of Cedar Hill. Secrecy met them at every turn. As the days passed on, the atmosphere became charged to its utmost with a current of mystery such as Merry Christmas had not brought for years.

On Christmas Eve there was a final rendezvous in the Davenport drawing room—a flurried, joyous bunch of 14 Cedar Hill young folks, whom James and Sis had pressed into service for the occasion.

They ranged in age from the youngest Ludington—a 5-year-old mannie in curls and kilts—to the Lee twins, just of age and decked in swallowtails and white shirt fronts. James, Jr., who had passed his twentieth birthday and overtopped the Lees by two inches, was master of ceremonies, and led proceedings in his gravely dignified way. Next to him was Isabelle Clyde, the tall blonde, beautiful in blue chiffon, and then Sis—black-crowned Sis, whose graceful ways and glorious blue-black hair were attractions that made one forget the color of her gown.

Hastily they stationed themselves in the front hall, the Lee twins, butler-wise at either side of the drawing room entrance ready to pull the curtains; James, Jr., and Sis waiting to receive, and the rest hustling to the place allotted to them, to tune their various instruments. There was indeed an orchestra. It consisted of one piano, one violin, four ukuleles, and three combs, well papered, well tuned.

What a travesty on the usual Davenport recital! Will the proud Cedar Hillites be game? Is the contrast too great? Is it indeed true that it does not rain Christmas festivities—that we must buy them? At this moment Sis turned an appealing glance toward James, Jr. Did he, too, feel the inadequacy of their attempt? But her brother's eyes were fixed toward the top of the carved oak staircase where his mother and father were descending, evidently determined to be game whatever the cost, and smilingly concealing any misgivings.

* * * * *

As they reached the hall below, Cordelia glanced at the floor. The rugs were gone, and from the big front door stretched a strip of canvas, fastened carefully with thumb tacks.

"What's this for?" she asked in surprise, turning to her son.

"We don't know, mother," James, Jr., told her with a grin. "Mr. Lee asked us to put it down."

"Mr. Lee!"

At that instant sounded a lugubrious thud on the front porch, followed by shouts of laughter. The door burst open, and in rushed Mr. Lee, Mr. Ludington, Mr. Clyde, and all the other guests, dragging a heavy weight across the mysterious canvas.

"Hello, Davenport! Got a place for this thing?"

"Oh, oh, a Yule log! All decorated with holly—how perfectly lovely! Wait, I'll help!"

Pushing and laughing, the orchestra piled into the hall to see.

"It ought to have come at sundown," explained Clyde, "but the invitation said eight o'clock, so—" He gave a final heave, and the huge thing settled into place, and the festive fire was lighted.

Never had the Davenport Christmas entertainment started in so unceremonious a fashion. The company stood about, talking excitedly, and not till the old Yule log was actually beginning to kindle did they go upstairs to remove their wraps.

Cordelia turned to Sis and James, Jr. "It's going to be perfectly splendid!" she said under her breath. "Your father and I almost worried, but they are taking it beautifully."

The music had begun—the violin wailed, the combs buzzed. Sis seized her mother's arm and pointed. Cordelia Davenport gasped. Down the staircase came Mr. and Mrs. Lee, arm in arm in solemnity unequaled, and behind them trooped the other guests, all arrayed in costumes the splendor of which no Davenport recital had ever witnessed. Mrs. Lee's gown was composed completely of ruffles from the Sunday comic section, in pink and red and blue. Her husband was in black and white, as became a gentleman, with narrow spiral ruffles of the *Daily Tribune* and the *Argus-Herald* incasing each leg and arm.

Were they game? Could anything in all the great town, with its wealth and pride, its poverty and greater pride, its struggles and sorrows, its jealousies and joys, equal the true Christmas spirit of haughty grandmother Ludington in her rustling gown of fine print "want ads"?

The youngest Ludington jumped before her and clapped his hands and cried, "O Gamma! Gamma!" and jumped again and lost his balance on the waxed floor, and had to be hugged and comforted.

The orchestra trembled and squeaked, and failed in laughter. The guests rustled and swished and laughed, while the Lee twins, faithful to their office, drew back the heavy crimson portieres and revealed the Christmas drawing room. There were no festoons of ground pine, no holly wreaths, not even the ancient bunch of mistletoe—but a blaze of glory that dazzled and blinded. The walls were lined with plate-glass mirrors, full length, expansive, reflecting and reflecting in bewildering infinity, multiplying a thousandfold the candles burning in Cordelia Davenport's cut-glass candlesticks. There was the big library mirror with its gilded frame, the mirrors from dining room, hall, and guest rooms, and all the family looking glasses—everything that would reflect. And in the center of the room, upon a tiny table, stood a diminutive Davenport Christmas tree, its tiny candles glittering and winking at their million reproductions reflected on every side. There were 50 Christmas trees—there were hundreds—thousands, it seemed! There were 25 guests—there were 50—there were 100!

And then the recital began with an opening chorus by the Cedar Hill, Jr., 14—a quaint old Christmas carol they had learned at school.

30

After the singing was over, Ludington turned to James, Sr.

"This is great!" he cried. "Why didn't we ever do it before? What's this, Sis? Going to give these to me?" he went on comically. She had paused before him with a silver tray of tiny cards.

Sis laughed. "No, sir. You may have just one. We're going to set you all to work. The card will tell you what to do."

"Number four! Number four! Where's number four?" called Archie Clyde, rushing frantically about.

"Oh, Isabelle, are you seven? You and I are to beat the eggs!"

"Number four—number four!"

James, Sr., roused. "What's all this about? Why, I'm number four—my card is marked four. Here, Archie, what do you want?"

The boy poised on one leg in front of him, and read from his card; "Help number four turn the freezers."

" 'When the gong sounds, lead the way to the kitchen,' " read Mrs. Lee, meditatively. "Why—where *is* the kitchen?"

Madam Ludington was adjusting her eyeglasses. "Here, somebody," she cried. "Do read my card for me!" She handed it to a curly-headed Ludington.

"Oh, Grandma! You are to cut the cake! Oh, isn't this fun? Wait—I'll tell you what it says. 'Please cut the cake, which you will find on the broad shelf in the serving room. There is a knife in the left-hand upper drawer of the kitchen cabinet.' "

"Oh," cried Madam, "how can I ever do anything in these paper furbelows?"

A gong sounded above the din. "Come on, everybody," called Mrs. Lee. "We're going to the kitchen!"

"The freezers are all packed. All you have to do is keep them rolling," explained James, Sr., to Archie, after an examination of the two rounded tubs, which seemed screwed to the table.

"Where's the egg beater? Where's the—"

"Doesn't it tell? Why, yes! 'On hanger above the sink.' Here it is!"

Such laughter, such informality, never had been known. The newspapered guests flew back and forth. They folded paper napkins, they arranged plates of cookies, they beat eggs, and turned them stiff and foaming into the lemon sherbet. They carried chairs, they drew water and filled glasses.

"I'm to light the candles on the cake," sang Mrs. Clyde, "but where are the matches?"

"Here—here—in this tin box!"

At last all was ready, and the company returned to the Christmas drawing room to eat what they themselves had served.

"You see, we couldn't have a caterer," Sis explained.

"Ladies and gentlemen!" the voice of James, Jr., rose above the din, and they looked to where he stood, straight and tall, between the bay windows. "Ladies and gentlemen. Twenty-five years ago tonight, on Cedar Hill, in the Davenport parlor, nine persons gathered to celebrate Christmas Eve. On that night a compact was made in the light of the Christmas candles to the effect that so long as they were neighbors, in sickness, or in health, in adversity as well as prosperity, they would, unless unavoidably prevented, spend each ensuing Christmas night together.

Those nine persons were Mr. and Mrs. Frank Clyde, Mr. and Mrs. Walter Lee, Mr. and Mrs. Eugene Ludington, Madam Ludington, and Mr. and Mrs. James Davenport.

"Wherefore we, the children and heirs of the aforesaid persons, have determined that, so long as the power within us lies, we will, with sincerity and good will to all, aid and abet the aforesaid persons, and if at any time their courage fails, or money is otherwise diverted, we will, by reason of our inherited ability and traditional inventiveness, provide such entertainment as may be needed for the annual occasion.

"In token whereof we present you with this birthday cake, holding 25 candles, each one of which represents a single Christmas celebration during the past quarter century. And," he added with a grin, "as there are now 25 of us, including two guests, there is just one piece apiece, with a candle for each!"

Cordelia Davenport's eyes glowed. She turned to her daughter.

"Oh, Sis!" she breathed, "how did you know? Who told you?"

"Madam Ludington. And oh, Mother, she's been just the best help! She suggested the paper costumes, too. Do look at her!"

The old lady was shaking with laughter, while she tried to repair a damaged paper flounce with pins.

And then, at last, amid the clamor of tongues there sounded distant sweet chords. Intrigued, the guests sought the source. In the music room the youngest Ludington, the little mannie in curls and kilts, stood by the grand piano looking at Sis. All the lanterns and candles but one had been extinguished. There was a sudden hush.

Sis played the opening chord of Martin Luther's beloved children's hymn, the child turned and began to sing:

"Away in a manger, no crib for a bed,
The little Lord Jesus laid down His sweet head.
The stars in the bright sky looked down where
He lay,
The little Lord Jesus asleep on the hay!"

Across the room where the singer gazed as he sang was a créche, illuminated by three candles. As the last notes died away into the night, there followed absolute silence.

Christ had returned to Cedar Hill Christmas.

The Gift of the Magi

O. Henry

Whenever Christmas stories are shared, there are a few (so few they may be counted on the fingers of one hand) that, like cream, invariably rise to the top. Very few stories survive the generation they are written for; and fewer yet are alive for a third. Thus, to be around for a fourth presupposes an intangible something that remains undefinable. Of these lonely holdouts none is more beloved than this story.

William Sidney Porter, of Greensboro, North Carolina, became famous as O. Henry, chronicling those people forgotten by the literati. Society columnists might glorify the "400" elite who were worthy to be invited to a Vanderbilt fete, but, to O. Henry, the really important New Yorkers were the 4,000,000 who weren't invited. Representative of these 4,000,000 are the young and so very poor Mr. and Mrs. James Dillingham Young. No more unlikely candidates to Magi-hood could one imagine.

One dollar and eighty-seven cents. That was all. And 60 cents of it was in pennies. Pennies saved one and two at a time by bulldozing the grocer and the vegetable man and the butcher until one's cheeks burned with the silent imputation of parsimony that such close dealing implied. Three times Della counted it. One dollar and eighty-seven cents. And the next day would be Christmas.

There was clearly nothing to do but flop down on the shabby little couch and howl. So Della did it. Which instigates the moral reflection that life is made up of sobs, sniffles, and smiles, with sniffles predominating.

While the mistress of the home is gradually subsiding from the first stage to the second, take a look at the home. A furnished flat at $8 per week. It did not exactly beggar description, but it certainly had that word on the lookout for the mendicancy squad.

In the vestibule below was a letter-box into which no letter would go, and an electric button from which no mortal finger could coax a ring. Also appertaining thereunto was a card bearing the name "Mr. James Dillingham Young."

The "Dillingham" had been flung to the breeze during a former period of prosperity when its possessor was being paid $30 per week. Now, when the income was shrunk to $20, the letters of "Dillingham" looked blurred, as though they were thinking seriously of contracting to a modest and unassuming D. But whenever Mr. James Dillingham Young came home and reached his flat above he was called "Jim" and greatly hugged by Mrs. James Dillingham Young, already introduced to you as Della. Which is all very good.

Della finished her cry and attended to her cheeks with the powder rag. She stood by the window and looked out dully at a gray cat walking a gray fence in a gray backyard. Tomorrow would be Christmas Day, and she had only $1.87 with which to buy Jim a present. She had been saving every penny she could for months, with this result. Twenty dollars a week doesn't go far. Expenses had been greater than she had calculated. They always are. Only $1.87 to buy a present for Jim. Her Jim. Many a happy hour she had spent planning for something nice for him. Something fine and rare and sterling—something just a little bit near to being worthy of the honor of being owned by Jim.

There was a pier glass between the windows of the room. Perhaps you have seen a pier glass in an $8 flat. A very thin and very agile person may, by observing his reflection in a rapid sequence of longitudinal strips, obtain a fairly accurate conception of his looks. Della, being slender, had mastered the art.

Suddenly she whirled from the window and stood before the glass. Her eyes were shining brilliantly, but her face had lost its color within 20 seconds. Rapidly she pulled down her hair and let it fall to its full length.

Now, there were two possessions of the James Dillingham Youngs in which they both took a mighty pride. One was Jim's gold watch that had been his father's and his grandfather's. The other was Della's hair. Had the Queen of Sheba lived in the flat across the airshaft, Della would have let her hair hang out the window some day to dry just to depreciate Her Majesty's jewels and gifts. Had King Solomon been the janitor, with all his treasures piled up in the basement, Jim would have pulled out his watch every time he passed, just to see him pluck at his beard from envy.

So now Della's beautiful hair fell about her rippling and shining like a cascade of brown waters. It reached below her knees and made itself almost a garment for her. And then she did it up again nervously and quickly. Once she faltered for a minute and stood still while a tear or two splashed on the worn red carpet.

On went her old brown jacket; on went her old brown hat. With a whirl of skirts and with the brilliant sparkle still in her eyes, she fluttered out the door and down the stairs to the street.

Where she stopped the sign read: "Mme. Sofronie. Hair Goods of All Kinds." One flight up Della ran, and collected herself, panting. Madame, large, too white, chilly, hardly looked the "Sofronie."

"Will you buy my hair?" asked Della.

"I buy hair," said Madame. "Take yer hat off and let's have a sight at the looks of it."

Down rippled the brown cascade.

"Twenty dollars," said Madame, lifting the mass with a practiced hand.

"Give it to me quick," said Della.

Oh, and the next two hours tripped by on rosy wings. Forget the hashed metaphor. She was ransacking the stores for Jim's present.

She found it at last. It surely had been made for Jim and no one else. There was no other like it in any of the stores, and she had turned all of them inside out. It was a platinum fob chain simple and chaste in design, properly proclaiming its value by substance alone and not by meretricious ornamentation—as all good things should do. It was even worthy of The Watch. As soon as she saw it she knew that it must be Jim's. It was like him. Quietness and value—the description applied to both. Twenty-one dollars they took from her for it, and she hurried home with the 87 cents. With that chain on his watch Jim might be properly anxious about the time in any company. Grand as the watch was, he sometimes looked at it on the sly on account of the old leather strap that he used in place of a chain.

When Della reached home her intoxication gave way a little to prudence and reason. She got out her curling irons and lighted the gas and went to work repairing the ravages made by generosity added to love. Which is always a tremendous task, dear friends—a mammoth task.

Within 40 minutes her head was covered with tiny, close-lying curls that made her look wonderfully like a truant schoolboy. She looked at her reflection in the mirror long, carefully, and critically.

"If Jim doesn't kill me," she said to herself, "before he takes a second look at me, he'll say I look like a Coney Island chorus girl. But what could I do—oh! what could I do with a dollar and eighty-seven cents?"

At 7 o'clock the coffee was made and the frying-pan was on the back of the stove hot and ready to cook the chops.

Jim was never late. Della doubled the fob chain in her hand and sat on the corner of the table near the door that he always entered. Then she heard his step on the stair away down on the first flight, and she turned white for just a moment. She had a habit of saying little silent prayers about the simplest everyday things, and now she whispered: "Please God, make him think I am still pretty."

The door opened and Jim stepped in and closed it. He looked thin and very serious. Poor fellow, he was only 22—and to be burdened with a family! He needed a new overcoat and he was without gloves.

Jim stopped inside the door, as immovable as a setter at the scent of quail. His eyes were fixed upon Della, and there was an expression in them that she could not read, and it terrified her. It was not anger, nor surprise, nor disapproval, nor horror, nor any of the sentiments that she had been prepared for. He simply stared at her fixedly with that peculiar expression on his face.

Della wriggled off the table and went for him.

"Jim, darling," she cried, "don't look at me that way. I had my hair cut off and sold it because I couldn't have lived through Christmas without giving you a present. It'll grow out again—you won't mind, will you? I just had to do it. My hair grows awfully fast. Say 'Merry Christmas!' Jim, and let's be happy. You don't know what a nice—what a beauti-ful nice gift I've got for you."

"You've cut off your hair?" asked Jim, laboriously, as if he had not arrived at that patent fact yet even after the hardest mental labor.

"Cut it off and sold it," said Della. "Don't you like me just as well, anyhow? I'm me without my hair, ain't I?"

Jim looked about the room curiously.

"You say your hair is gone?" he said, with an air almost of idiocy.

"You needn't look for it," said Della. "It's sold, I tell you—sold and gone, too. It's Christmas Eve, boy. Be good to me, for it went for you. Maybe the hairs of my head were numbered," she went on with a sudden serious sweetness, "but nobody could ever count my love for you. Shall I put the chops on, Jim?"

Out of his trance Jim seemed quickly to wake. He enfolded his Della. For 10 seconds let us regard with discreet scrutiny some inconsequential object in the other direction. Eight dollars a week or a million a year—what is the difference? A mathematician or a wit would give you the wrong answer. The magi brought valuable gifts, but that was not among them. This dark assertion will be illuminated later on.

Jim drew a package from his overcoat pocket and threw it upon the table.

"Don't make any mistake, Dell," he said, "about me. I don't think there's anything in the way of a haircut or a shave or a shampoo that could make me like my girl any less. But if you'll unwrap that package you may see why you had me going a while at first."

White fingers and nimble tore at the string and paper. And then an ecstatic scream of joy; and then, alas! a quick feminine change to hysterical tears and wails, necessitating the immediate employment of all the comforting powers of the lord of the flat.

For there lay The Combs—the set of combs, side and back, that Della had worshipped for long in a Broadway window. Beautiful combs, pure tortoise shell, with jeweled rims—just the shade to wear in the beautiful vanished hair. They were expensive combs, she knew, and her heart had simply craved and yearned over them without the least hope of possession. And now, they were hers, but the tresses that should have adorned the coveted adornments were gone.

But she hugged them to her bosom, and at length she was able to look up with dim eyes and a smile and say: "My hair grows so fast, Jim!"

And then Della leaped up like a little singed cat and cried, "Oh, oh!"

Jim had not yet seen his beautiful present. She held it out to him eagerly upon her open palm. The dull precious metal seemed to flash with a reflection of her bright and ardent spirit.

"Isn't it a dandy, Jim? I hunted all over town to find it. You'll have to look at the time a hundred times a day now. Give me your watch. I want to see how it looks on it."

Instead of obeying, Jim tumbled down on the couch and put his hands under the back of his head and smiled.

"Dell," he said, "let's put our Christmas presents away and keep 'em a while. They're too nice to use just at present. I sold the watch to get the money to buy your combs. And now suppose you put the chops on."

The magi, as you know, were wise men—wonderfully wise men—who brought gifts to the Babe in the manger. They invented the art of giving Christmas presents. Being wise, their gifts were no doubt wise ones, possibly bearing the privilege of exchange in case of duplication. And here I have lamely related to you the uneventful chronicle of two foolish children in a flat who most unwisely sacrificed for each other the greatest treasures of their house. But in a last word to the wise of these days let it be said that of all who give gifts these two were the wisest. Everywhere they are wisest. They are the Magi.

Running Away From Christmas

Annie Hamilton Donnell

Have you ever felt like running away from Christmas, to a place where there is no evidence that it even exists? Well, that's the way Katharine Kane felt, so she abducted her long-suffering husband, Anthony, and they fled—with entirely unexpected and far-reaching results. Almost 100 years ago, it was—but it might just as well have been today.

Sit down, Anthony, right here on the hall bench, before you take off your coat. Dinner isn't ready, anyway, and I've time to tell you something. It's—it's my ultimatum. I think that's what you call it."

The face of Anthony Kane, softened and stirred by his wife's kiss, stiffened into astonishment. What was this Kitty had to say solemn enough to merit "Anthony" and "ultimatum"? Kitty rarely greeted him with big words.

"You needn't be scared, dear, though *I* am! I frighten myself—but I shall do it. I have spent all day deciding: and you know, when I *decide*, Anthony—"

"Oh, come, call me by my right name!"

"Well, Tony, then. Sit down. You look so big standing up, and I feel specially little with this on my mind. Tony, we'll run away from Christmas."

"We'll—what?"

"Run away. It will be simple enough; only we must run in time. I've got our things nearly packed. You needn't say a syllable." Her cool fingers were over his lips. "I'm doing the saying. I have it all planned right down to the single detail of where to run to. It's got to be some place where there isn't a thought of Christmas; that's all I stipulate. We'll keep on running till we get to That Place."

"Katharine!"

"Call me Kitty. Yes, dear?"

"You never told me there was insanity in your family. This isn't giving a fellow a square deal."

"Well, there is insanity," returned his small, cool wife. "It comes on periodically. We are all taken crazy just about this time o' year, and we gradually recover after Christmas. This year I am going to skip my attack. And you've got to 'skip' with me." She laughed enjoyingly at her modest pun. Her hand crossed and recrossed Anthony Kane's shaven cheek, with the lingering and tender touch of childless wives who have so much time to caress husbands' cheeks.

"Think of not having to do up the bundles, Tony, not one bundle! No flurry and scurry and scolding each other at the last minute; no tissue paper and ribbon and strings and writing addresses. Just you and me"—Kitty was not always hampered by grammatic rule—"sitting comfortably together in That Place, wherever it is, the No-Christmas Place we are going to run away to."

He attempted to restore her sanity by homely suggestion. "Let's run away to dinner," he soothed. "If I'm not mistaken, I smell a Belinda potpie—"

"We'll start anyway, day after tomorrow. I suppose you will have to have time to wind up your affairs. Tony, if I never had an inspiration before, this is one. And to think of all the dreading and planning I might have saved! I spent *hours* trying to reckon how we stand with the Smith-Curtises, and what we'd got to spend on the Dana Wards this year."

She sprang lightly to her feet, and faced him.

"Christmas!" she scorned, all her sweet face aflame. "Merry Christmas! Anthony Kane, we've been married 11 years, 11 weary Christmases full of nervous prostration, and empty pocketbooks, and—and tissue paper, and *strings!* Trying to keep up our end of things and give folks as valuable presents as they gave us last year! I don't know what you call it; I call it a give-and-take scramble, and I've had enough of it. There's no way out of it but to run away. I don't want to see or hear a word of Christmas, and there must be a place somewhere. We'll take hold of hands, dear, and find it. Now we'll have dinner."

But she drifted back to him as he hung up his coat. The tone that penetrated into that little closet was a tone he knew, but rarely had heard. He did not need to look at Kitty's broken little face.

"Of course—of course I'd have *loved* Christmas if we'd ever hung up little stockings; do you think I'd run away from that?" And she was gone again. There had never been little stockings.

Two days later they were actually on their way to That Place beyond the reach of Christmas. It was characteristic of Katharine Kane that the wild little plan had materialized; she was accustomed to carry through her plans. To Anthony Kane, her husband, to whom she was wife and children and all the world, submission even to crazy little schemes came easily. He had, fortunately, leisure and wherewithal to indulge her.

"Well, we've started for somewhere, Puss, but how do you know you won't find a Christmas there? We may run right into it."

"Don't laugh; this is sober earnest. Honestly, Tony, I am so sick of the present-day mercenary, distorted kind of celebrating that I want to *rest*; yes, I do! I want to forget it. You're a dear, not to mind anything, not even being pulled up by the roots at a moment's notice. When I get home, I shall give *you* a Christmas present." The inconsistency of woman!

"But just now we are on the way to a place called Hardscrabble. I picked it out on a timetable. You don't look for a Christmas there, do you?" She laughed, not without modest pride at her "find."

"But if anything happens that we 'run into' one, as you predict, I've two other promising places on my list: Starkville and World's End—what do you say to going to those? The last one isn't on a railroad; we'll have to hire a sleigh and hunt it up. I happened to see a reference to it in the newspaper. Oh, Tony, aren't you beginning to have a lovely time? Just us two!"

"Great! Real Christmas spirit," mumbled Tony. He was in reality not averse to this remarkable escapade. He and Kitty deserved a little freedom after their 11 proper and expensive Christmases.

He did not really accept her pessimistic theory of the utter demoralization of Christmas; in Anthony Kane's still youthful mind were too many blissful memories, but he "accepted" Kitty. Poor child, she had been a little solitary up to the time he had found her; and from that time on had occurred the wearisome annual games of give and take that had occasioned this adventurous quest. Kitty had much to excuse her. He never forgot the denied sweets of motherhood that she had missed.

"But look here." It was considerably further on in the trip; an uncomfortable thought had just occurred to him. "Kitty, how will it look?"

"Look? Oh, Tony, you waked me up, and I was starting in on such a beautiful dream! How will what look, dear?"

"This—this freak of ours. Everybody'll send us the costly rubbish just the same. I don't like the taste of the thought, Katharine."

"I've fixed that part, of course. We shall not find the front porch piled with bundles, man, dear; go on with your newspaper. I dropped a hint with Celia Beede, and I waited till she picked it up, too. Celia is so dependable!"

Hardscrabble proved a sightly little town set on a hill. It had a suspicious look of a certain amount of thrift and cheer, even in the gloom of its ill-lighted little streets. They were driven in silence to its one hotel, Katharine's spirits oddly damped. Well, all there was about it—there were the two other places! She would put into immediate action her investigations. If Hardscrabble proved a disappointment—it was destined to do it.

After the ambitious little meal called "supper," Katharine disappeared. It was half an hour later when she broke in upon Anthony sitting in the hot little bedroom.

"Oh, you've got your coat off! Put it on quick; our train goes in 15 minutes! There's a sleeper on it. You shall have a good night's rest, poor boy. I'm doing the best I can for you."

"But what—"

"We can't stay here, Tony. This place is *full* of Christmas! I've been out investigating. The shop windows are all lighted up and decorated—actually decorated! And about every house has Christmas wreaths in the windows. Hurry, dear! I'll shut up the bags."

At Starkville, when by devious ways they finally arrived at that dreary-sounding place, they were met upon the little station platform with no less than three "Merry Christmases." More of them, cheery and friendly, greeted them at the Starkville House. It appeared to be a Christmassy little spot.

"Now, isn't it too bad? You'll have to put up with a top-floor room, and a back one at that! But we're full, because of Christmas. The band folks always put up with us, and we always have a band here for the rally."

" 'Rally?' " but Katharine did not look at Anthony. Already she tasted new defeat. In a species of despair she clutched Anthony's arm and walked out.

"Never mind, Puss; better luck next time," comforted that soothing person. "There's your third place—End o' the World, is it? We haven't given that a trial. If we run into Christmas there, we'll change our tactics and call it our wedding trip. We never really had one, and it's nobody's business when or where we go."

"Oh, you're a dear!" she sighed. "No other woman's husband would have come off like this, anyway, just to please a frantic wife."

Kitty was travel-worn and in her secret soul a little repentant of her lunacy. Even a Christmas-harried, bundle-littered home looked appealing to her tonight. But because she was Kitty it did not occur to her to turn back from her undertaking. She had undertaken to find a Christmasless place and spend her Christmas in it. Besides, she hadn't run away from Tony.

"Let's have supper," she cried briskly. "Let's be happy, dear! Just us two at a little table here at the end of the world. Then we'll go to the real World's End. We're *due* there, Tony. You don't mind?"

"Me, mind?" Tony was just getting into the spirit of things. He had the windy little sense of having eloped with Kitty; and the farther they ran, the better. Had he ever really had her to himself before?

After supper they continued their adventurous journeying to World's End.

"I think," Kitty mused aloud, "that we've been harnessed up, with the overdraw checkrein and all that, you know, and driven in little narrow roads that other people made for us, and we didn't dare to turn out of. We're—we're unchecked now, and—out to grass!" She laughed enjoyingly. "Doesn't it seem good to get our heads down, and *browse?*" He stooped suddenly and kissed her.

World's End had been properly named; but they succeeded in finding it, and the night before Christmas found them in the primitive little settlement of a half dozen houses and a blacksmith shop. That round a bend in the road a little farther on they would have found more houses and a general store they refused to be told; this was the World's End they wanted. It satisfied Kitty; she saw no signs of Christmas.

The elderly soul in one of the houses, who agreed to take them in, did not wish them a merry Christmas. The elderly man soul who appeared to belong to her wore a serious, un-Christmas countenance. There were no holly wreaths visible anywhere, and the blacksmith shop was undecorated.

"We've found the Place," Kitty whispered, but she boasted too soon. Two hours later she realized her mistake.

Tony had gone to bed in the company room of the little house; but Kitty, with a woman's uneasiness and her own particular gift of wakefulness, had remained up with a book from one of the suitcases.

"Tony—Tony!" Her lips were close to his ear, and she was gently shaking him. She had just returned from a little excursion to the kitchen for a drink.

"Tony, they've hung their stockings up—their poor old stockings!" Kitty was crying, though she did not know it, and could scarcely have told why, if she had known. "Get up, dear. Tony, please! Help me find something nice of yours for the solemn old man-stocking. I know of something for the other one."

So it came about that a few minutes later these two who had run away from Christmas, stole, stocking-footed, out to the small, drear kitchen to play Santa Claus.

"Let a little end hang over the top, so he'll see it first thing. It's your prettiest tie; Tony, you're a dear; Tony, if you dare to laugh at me!" but he was not laughing.

As they sat at breakfast the next morning, a little trail of humble vehicles paraded past the window; and the old person waiting upon them explained it. She was suddenly excited.

"Ezry! Ezry! It's goin' past! Don't stop to wipe your face!" she called to her old husband in a room beyond. "It's Mis' Blacksmith Avery, her that was young Ellen Till," she explained to her guests. "Isn't it a pity to be buried on Christmas day? And Blacksmith Avery *Thanksgiving!* I tell *him* it should have been us; we wouldn't have left two little mites."

"Oh, two little mites!" breathed Kitty. Her fork slipped with a soft clatter to her plate. She sat forward in her chair, her eyes on the tail of the somber little procession going by.

"Two, yes; I suppose it's a mercy there weren't six; but I declare it's hard to see some mercies. They're little dears; Ellen was a beautiful girl. There isn't any better stock anywhere round here than Till stock, and I don't know but Avery comes next. I have never seen politer little dears."

"Oh—little dears!" Kitty murmured. Tony did not venture to look at the troubled little face of her.

He felt the stirrings of her denied and hungry soul.

The old voice ran on garrulously. It was rare it found so good a chance as this.

"Fond o' children, are you?" The old eyes had come to rest on Kitty's face. "Well, then, I guess you'd be fond o' these children! If you'd like to see them, I'll go over with you. The poor farm's coming after them this afternoon. We better go soon."

But Kitty had already gone, alone. The old woman's gaze followed her admiringly.

"Isn't she spry? Well, I tell him to look at the way I used to go around instead of looking at me now. Yes, we've got to let the poor farm take the Blacksmith Avery children." She sighed. "There is no one else to take them, and there isn't a grain of money to keep them if there was. 'Twon't be much different for them, poor dears, than for the rest of us. All of us live on poor farms."

Anthony Kane was not surprised that Kitty did not come back alone. He went a little way along the snowy road to meet her, and now he looked at Kitty's face. It was lighted softly by some inner light, the light he knew.

"This is 'Son,' and this is 'Sister,'" she introduced quietly. "They are both so little, Tony!"

"Sister is; I ain't. I'm big," the little voice of Son piped eagerly. "When I'm 'leven months older, I'll be 7. I—I mean I was *goin'* to be if Mother hadn't died."

"I want Mother!" suddenly broke in baby wailing from the tremulous lips of the other child. Sister in 'leven months more could not be more than 4. Her round, wholesome little face was grotesquely con-torted with its grief. To Anthony Kane, looking down, it was a piteous little face.

"Man, dear—"

"Yes, Puss—yes, I know."

"Both, Anthony? How can a little Son live without a little Sister?"

But he was spared decision. Son was before him.

"She's goin' to take me, an' I'm goin' to take Sister, an' we're goin' to have a Chris'mas. You tell him," pushing Kitty forward. "Tell him he can kiss Sister; the best place is under her chin."

To Tony, Son gravely explained: "I promised to let her kiss me 'leven more months, but she better do it on my hair; that's the cleanest place. Can I pray Sister nights? I promised mother I would."

Katharine Kane on her knees gathered the two of them into her arms. It was as if they were "praying" her. A long time afterward—it seemed—she heard Anthony's voice, striving for matter-of-factness.

"There's a train on that little branch at one o'clock. If we could catch it—"

"Of course we can catch it! If we have to run all the four miles! We've got to hurry home, Tony, on account of Christmas. We'll be a day or two late, but we'll catch it!"

She dropped her voice to an eager whisper. "Little stockings," she breathed. "We've got to hurry home and hang them up."

And again they were off, but this time, they were running after Christmas.

The Last Straw

Paula McDonald Palangi

One of the most beautiful Christmas stories of the 1970s was written about a quarreling family and what the mother did to restore a sense of caring to their familial relationships. I feel that this particular story will wear very well down through the years, and will be with us for a long time.

Initially, this story was scheduled to be included in our first collection but, in courtesy to Cathy Davis, editor at David C. Cook, and the special illustrated version of the story Cook published in the fall of 1992 (it includes a cardboard pull-out cradle), inclusion was delayed until this collection.

To truly share this season of love and laughter, even a little boy must first discover Christmas in his heart.

Everyone, unfortunately, was cooped up in the house that typical gray winter afternoon. And, as usual, the four little McNeals were at it again, teasing each other, squabbling, bickering, always fighting over their toys.

At times like this, Ellen was almost ready to believe that her children didn't love each other, even though she knew that wasn't true. All brothers and sisters fight sometimes, of course, but lately her lively little bunch had been particularly horrid to each other, especially Eric and Kelly, who were only a year apart. The two of them seemed determined to spend the whole long winter making each other miserable.

"Give me that. It's mine!" Kelly screamed, her voice shrill.

"It is not! I had it first," Eric answered stubbornly.

Ellen sighed as she listened to the latest argument. With Christmas only a month away, the house seemed sadly lacking in Christmas spirit.

This was supposed to be the season of sharing and love, of warm feelings and happy hearts. A home needed more than just pretty packages and twinkling lights on a tree to fill the holidays with joy.

Ellen had only one idea. Years ago, her grandmother had told her about an old custom that helped people discover the true meaning of Christmas. Perhaps it would work for her family this year. It was certainly worth a try.

She gathered the children together and lined them up on the couch, tallest to smallest—Eric, Kelly, Lisa, and Mike.

"How would you kids like to start a new Christmas tradition this year?" she asked. "It's like a game, but it can be played only by people who can keep a secret. Can everyone here do that?"

"I can!" shouted Eric.

"I can keep a secret better than him!" yelled Kelly.

"I can do it!" chimed in Lisa.

"Me too. Me too," squealed little Mike. "I'm big enough."

"Well then, this is how the game works," Ellen explained. "This year we're going to surprise Baby Jesus when He comes on Christmas Eve by making Him the softest bed in the world. We're going to fill a little crib with straw to make it comfortable. But here's the secret part. The straw we put in will measure the good deeds we've done, but we won't tell anyone who we're doing them for."

The children looked confused. "But how will Jesus know it's His bed?" Kelly asked.

"He'll know," said Ellen. "He'll recognize it by the love we put in to make it soft."

"But who will we do the good deeds for?" asked Eric, still a little confused.

"We'll do them for each other. Once a week we'll put all of our names in a hat, mine and Daddy's too. Then we'll each pick out a different name. Whosever name we draw, we'll do kind things for that person for a whole week. But you can't tell anyone else whose name you've chosen. We'll each try to do as many favors for our special person as we can without getting caught. And for every good deed we do, we'll put another straw in the crib."

"Like being a spy!" squealed Lisa.

"But what if I pick someone's name that I don't like?" Kelly frowned.

Ellen thought about that for a minute. "Maybe you could use an extra fat piece of straw. And think how much faster the fat straws will fill up our crib. We'll use the cradle in the attic," she said. "And we can all go to the field behind the school for the straw."

Without a single argument, the children bundled into their wool hats and mittens, laughing and tumbling out of the house. The field had been covered with tall grass in summer, but now, dead and dried, the golden stalks looked just like real straw. They carefully selected handfuls and placed them in the large box they had carried with them.

"That's enough," Ellen laughed when the box was almost overflowing. "Remember, it's only a small cradle."

So home they went to spread their straw carefully on a large tray Ellen never used. Eric, because he was the eldest, was given the responsibility of climbing into the attic and bringing down the cradle.

"We'll pick names as soon as Daddy comes home for dinner," Ellen said, unable to hide a smile at the thought of Mark's pleased reaction to the children's transformed faces and their voices, filled now with excited anticipation rather than annoyance.

At the supper table that night, six pieces of paper were folded, shuffled and shaken around in Mark's furry winter hat, and the drawing began. Kelly picked a name first and immediately started to giggle. Lisa reached into the hat next, trying hard to look like a serious spy. Mike couldn't read yet, so Mark whispered the name in his ear. Then Mike quickly ate his little wad of paper so no one would ever learn the identity of his secret person. Eric was the next person to choose, and as he unfolded his scrap of paper, a frown creased his forehead. But he stuffed the name quickly into his pocket and said nothing. Ellen and Mark selected names and the family was ready to begin.

The week that followed was filled with surprises. It seemed the McNeal house had suddenly been invaded by an army of invisible elves. Kelly would walk into her room at bedtime to find her nightgown neatly laid out and her bed turned down. Someone cleaned up the sawdust under the workbench without being asked. The jelly blobs magically disappeared from the kitchen counter after lunch one day while Ellen was out getting the mail. And every morning, when Eric was brushing his teeth, someone crept quietly into his room and made the bed. It wasn't made perfectly, but it was made. That particular little elf must have had short arms because he couldn't seem to reach the middle.

"Where are my shoes?" Mark asked one morning. No one seemed to know, but suddenly, before he left for work, they were back in the closet again, freshly shined.

Ellen noticed other changes during that week, too. The children weren't teasing or fighting as much. An argument would start, and then suddenly stop right in the middle for no apparent reason. Even Eric and Kelly seemed to be getting along better and bickering less. In fact, there were times when all the

TOT'S HOME

children could be seen smiling secret smiles and giggling to themselves. And slowly, one by one, the first straws began to appear in the little crib. Just a few, then a few more each day. By the end of the first week, a little pile had accumulated.

Everyone was anxious to pick new names, and this time there was more laughter and merriment than there had been the first time. Except for Eric. Once again, he unfolded his scrap of paper, glanced at it, and stuffed it in his pocket without a word.

The second week brought more astonishing events, and the little pile of straw in the manger grew higher and softer. There was more laughter, less teasing, and hardly any arguments could be heard around the house. Only Eric had been unusually quiet, and sometimes Ellen would catch him looking a little sad. But the straws in the manger continued to pile up.

At last, it was almost Christmas. They chose names for the final time on the night before Christmas Eve. As they sat around the table waiting for the last set of names to be shaken in the hat, the children smiled as they looked at their hefty pile of straws. They all knew it was comfortable and soft, but there was one day left and they could still make it a little deeper, a little softer, and they were going to try.

For the last time the hat was passed around the table. Mike picked out a name, and again quickly ate the paper as he had done each week. Lisa unfolded hers carefully under the table, peeked at it and then hunched up her little shoulders, smiling. Kelly reached into the hat, and grinned from ear to ear

when she saw the name. Ellen and Mark each took their turn and handed the hat with the last name to Eric. As he unfolded the scrap of paper and glanced at it, his face crumpled and he seemed about to cry. Without a word, he turned and ran from the room.

Everyone immediately jumped up from the table, but Ellen stopped them. "No! Stay where you are," she said firmly. "I'll go."

In his room, Eric was trying to pull on his coat with one hand while he picked up a small cardboard suitcase with the other.

"I have to leave," he said quietly through his tears. "If I don't, I'll spoil Christmas."

"But why? And where are you going?"

"I can sleep in my snow fort for a couple of days. I'll come home right after Christmas, I promise."

Ellen started to say something about freezing and snow and no mittens or boots, but Mark, who had come up behind her, gently laid his hand on her arm and shook his head. The front door closed, and together they watched from the window as the little figure with the sadly slumped shoulders trudged across the street and sat down on a snowbank near the corner. It was dark outside, and cold, and a few flurries drifted down on the small boy and his suitcase.

"Give him a few minutes alone," said Mark quietly. "I think he needs that. Then you can talk to him."

The huddled figure was already dusted with white when Ellen walked across the street and sat down beside him on the snowbank.

"What is it, Eric? You've been so good these last few weeks, but I know something's been bothering you since we first started the crib. Can you tell me, honey?"

"Ah, Mom . . . don't you see?" He sniffed. "I tried so hard, but I can't do it anymore, and now I'm going to wreck Christmas for everybody." With that, he burst into sobs and threw himself into his mother's arms.

"Mom." The little boy choked. "You just don't know. I got Kelly's name every time! And I hate Kelly! I tried, Mom. I really did. I snuck in her room every night and fixed her bed. I even laid out her crummy nightgown. I let her use my race car one day, but she smashed it right into the wall like always! Every week, when we picked new names, I thought it would be over. Tonight, when I got her name again, I knew I couldn't do it anymore. If I try, I'll probably punch her instead. If I stay home and beat Kelly up, I'll spoil Christmas for everybody."

The two of them sat there together quietly for a few minutes and then Ellen spoke softly. "Eric, I'm so proud of you. Every good deed you did should count double because it was hard for you to be nice to Kelly for so long. But you did those good deeds anyway, one straw at a time. You gave your love when it wasn't easy to give. And maybe that's what the spirit of Christmas is really all about. And maybe it's the hard good deeds and the difficult straws that make that little crib special. You're the one who's probably added the most important straws this year."

Ellen paused, stroking the head pressed tightly against her shoulder. "Now, how would you like a chance to earn a few easy straws like the rest of us? I still have the name I picked in my pocket, and I haven't looked at it yet. Why don't we switch, for the last day? And it will be our secret."

Eric lifted his head and looked into her face, his eyes wide. "That's not cheating?"

"It's not cheating." And together they dried the tears, brushed off the snow, and walked back to the house.

The next day, the whole family was busy cooking and straightening up the house for Christmas Day, wrapping last-minute presents and trying hard to keep from bursting with excitement. But even with all the activity and eagerness, a flurry of new straws piled up in the crib, and by nightfall the little manger was almost overflowing. At different times while passing by, each member of the family, big and small, would pause and look at the wondrous pile for a moment, then smile before going on. But . . . who could really know? One more straw still might make a difference.

For that reason, just before bedtime, Ellen tiptoed quietly to Kelly's room to lay out the little blue nightgown and turn down the bed. But she stopped in the doorway, surprised. Someone had already been there. The nightgown was laid across the bed, and a small red race car had been placed next to it on the pillow.

The last straw was Eric's, after all.

Have You Seen the Star?

Margaret Slattery

This turn-of-the-century story is as powerful now as when it was first written. The question, "Have you seen the star?" takes on new meaning in Margaret Slattery's story: not the mere visual experience, but a much deeper, life-changing one.

The origins of the story are obscure; however, one thing is certain—it deserves to live on.

Fourth floor, please." Mrs. Carston left the elevator and walked down the broad aisle between toy motor cars, toy rocking horses, dolls, and games. She stopped beside the rail that enclosed the square set apart for the children, where attendants helped them into marvelous wings, lifted them to the backs of camels, elephants, or horses on the merry-go-round, or let them sail tiny boats on a miniature sea.

The young woman stood fascinated.

This would be the third year that she had spent a morning before that rail. The joyous laughter and those happy faces brought back the memories of her own little boy who was just 5 years old last month. It seemed cruel that the man who had been her husband should have this child at Christmas, yet she could not bear to think of the long summer days by the lake without his smiling face and the warm caress of his chubby hands. Three years it had been since the court had decided that Father and Mother might live apart but should share the boy for equal periods of six months. Now he had the boy, and it was only a few days before Christmas.

Of course, her boy would not be there in a public play room, but she liked to find the boys who resembled him. Watching them at their play, she suddenly realized that she was sobbing and laughing, then crying and laughing at the same time and not able to stop. A woman in a white uniform led her away to the emergency room where, after what seemed a long rest, the nurse asked if she had lost a child. The question revived her. Those people had no right to know. She said she felt better and ordered a taxi to take her home.

When she had taken off her wraps and thrown herself upon the couch, she told her faithful maid that she had become exhausted while in one of the stores and would have a light lunch served there in her room before trying to sleep. She half heard the words of sympathy, the scolding for doing too much, but the caress and the careful arrangement of pillows were a comfort. After the lunch, she tried in vain to sleep. Wandering about the room, her eyes fell on a little red book that she had thrown on the table a week before.

A friend had persuaded her to attend a tabernacle service. At the close of the meeting, a young woman with a most attractive face had given her the little book, saying, "Will you not read it sometime, please?" She had smiled and had said yes, but had not done it. Now she opened the little book, and lying down again, began to read the verses marked in red.

Utterly worn out by the strain of the morning, she did not read long, but closing her eyes, thought over the words. The rain that had been threatening all day began to fall and the room grew dark. Turning her face toward the wall she finally slept.

In her dream she found herself mixed up with a large procession of every sort of people who were rushing along a great highway toward a soft gray curtain of cloud that hid the sky. Where it touched the earth, a man stood with a long robe and with a wonderful face.

"Where are you all going?" she asked those by her side.

A gray-haired woman responded, "To see the star. It is the Bethlehem star, you know. They say that if you can see it, your mind and heart will be at peace and you will be happy the rest of your life."

The younger woman looked at the unhappy faces about her and then said, "I will walk along with you; we all look as though we need something to make us happy."

After a long time, she found herself before the man with the wonderful face and his keen eyes looked her through. "Would you see the star?"

"Yes, I want peace of mind and heart. I need it."

"Will you pay? It is a costly star."

"What must I pay?" she asked fearfully.

"Will you try to forgive him?" he asked so softly that no one else could hear.

"Oh, not that," she cried. "Anything but that."

"It is that price you must pay to see the star and know its peace."

But she shook her head and slowly joined the company of disappointed seekers who were going down the hill. Tears filled her eyes as she stumbled along. On the great plain below, she saw men lying dead in the snow, hundreds of them, the smoke of burning cities and the blaze of bursting shells. A voice seemed to say, "If only those who have brought men to this could see the star, peace would come to earth. But it is a costly star and they will not pay."

Failing to locate the speaker, she walked on and after a long time sat down to rest. There at the foot of the hill was a brightly lighted home. Before the fireplace a man and woman stood facing each other with hate and anger deforming their faces. A moment more and the man flung himself furiously into his coat and left the house. Again the mysterious voice remarked, "They need to see the star, but they will not pay. Neither can put himself in the place of the other. See, see the scores of wrecked homes—little children in them suffering the penalty. Selfishness has made both men and women deaf and blind."

Scorched by the words that seemed to touch her inmost soul, she cried out, "Lead me back; I must go back; I must see the star."

"You called? Did you want anything? It sounded as if you were in pain." The maid stood at the door, anxious and troubled.

"No," she answered. "I must have dreamed. I am glad you wakened me. Frank and Louise are coming for dinner and I'll have to dress at once."

Contrary to her usual dread of spending an evening alone, she longed to have her friends leave soon so that she might be able to think. When at last the good-nights had been said, she hurried to her room, undressed quickly, and turned on her bed lamp to read the Testament again. How many times she had read all night, seeking to drown memories that would not let her sleep—but never words like these. She had never taken religion very seriously. The life of the One who began in that manger to which the thoughts of millions would turn on Christmas morning and ended in the day's agony on a cross, and the glory of the open tomb, had never before deeply impressed her. But now she closed the book and turned out the light, conscious of an unseen and sympathetic presence.

In the dark she began to think of the days when James Carston had told her that he loved her. Then her wedding, the first year in his father's home, the misunderstanding—then the baby. Crowding upon each other came the memories of the things that she had said to him the day the child was a year old—of the words of cold disdain with which he had met her storms of anger.

"He should have been more patient," but now the words of the dream came hauntingly: "Neither can put himself in the other's place. Selfishness has made both men and women deaf and blind." Memories of the child came rushing over her—the last awful scene when the man had begged her to try again, to make one more attempt to understand him.

He had said he would do anything to save them (for the child's sake) from the publicity of separation, but she had answered that she would never forgive him and that she would relieve him of the burden of both herself and the child. She had meant then to take her little 2-year-old son and go back to her own home, but the court had said no.

All their quarrels had started with such little things, but how the memories hurt! Forgive him? It was the price of the star! Then she would never see it . . . The loneliness and longing would not be banished, for she could not fight it off with hard and bitter thoughts as before. Finally, in the gray light of early morning, she rose and knelt by the bed. After a long time she said slowly and aloud to the Presence, "Show me the star—I will pay—I will *try* to forgive him. I will forgive. Help me!" It was her first prayer.

51

Into her heart came the sense of peace. Comforted and conscious of sustaining strength, she went back to bed. The stars were fading. One seemed brighter than the other, and watching it, she fell asleep.

While Alma Carston had been dressing for dinner and trying in vain to shake herself free from her dream, the man who had been her partner in what he often sarcastically called the disillusionment, sat in his living room with his little son upon his knee.

The child had been saying a piece that he was to repeat with the other children at a Christmas service. With expression and accuracy that would have done credit to a person much older than just 5, he said the words of the first Christmas story. His aunt had taught it to him carefully but refused to answer any questions about the things she taught, and this evening a whole volley of them followed the recitation of the piece. Angels and wise men, shepherds and camels, mangers, gold, frankincense and myrrh, all came in for their share; and the questionnaire ended with three important questions: "Did you ever see the star, Daddy?" "Have you ever looked for it?" "Wouldn't you like to see it?"

Negative answers came from the man whose thoughts flew back over the years to the day when he himself stumbled through the words, "We have seen His star in the East and are come to worship Him." The child soon changed the subject, and shaking the father by his shoulders, demanded, "Tell me, Daddy, am I going to have a Christmas tree? Am I?"

"Sure, sure you are—a big tree that will touch the ceiling this year, since you are a big boy."

"What will be on it?"

"What do you want on it?"

The boy did not hesitate for a moment. He had evidently thought it over before. When, breathless, the boy finished, his father exclaimed, "One tree? You will need a forest of Christmas trees."

"Who is going to come to my tree, Daddy? The big cousins who came last year—will they come?"

"Yes, we'll ask anybody you want."

"Truly? Will we, Daddy?" He snuggled down into his father's arms and played with the fingers of the hand that held him tightly. He was silent so long that his father said, "Well, have you decided who you want?"

"Yes," the child answered, "I want Mother. Last Christmas she didn't have any tree. I asked her in the summer. She had only presents—she liked mine the best, but she didn't have any candy—nobody gave her any. Daddy, I wish you and Mother lived in the same house. Helen's daddy and her mother live in the same house, and so do Allen's," he sighed. "I asked Mother all summer to come and see us and she has never come. She's got lovely sunshine hair and she can swim fine. She taught me, only I can't do it yet."

He was still a moment or two and then added, "I guess I'll ask Carl. He's a scout. That'll be enough. She can tell stories lots better than Auntie and better than you, Daddy. Maybe she'll tell one an—" His aunt interrupted by saying that it was past time for bed

52

and Daddy's dinner was ready. The child seldom spoke of his mother, for he found that no one answered, and a strange uncomfortable feeling always followed the mention of her name. But having started talking about her, he found it very hard to stop and protested vigorously as his aunt led him away.

James Carston did not eat very heartily and he was not in a talkative mood. "Sunshine hair." He had told her that very thing himself. He remembered the day on the lake and the look with which she answered him. And he had taught her to swim. She was so vigorous that she had soon surpassed her teacher.

Immediately after dinner, he left for the mid-week service of the church in which he was an officer. When his father had died, the whole congregation had mourned the loss of their most prominent member and real friend, and they had persuaded him to take his father's place. Of late, he had often tried to give it up, but they would not listen to it. Usually he did not attend the weekly service, but tonight his presence had been requested, for over a hundred people were to seek membership in the church—the largest number that had ever come before it.

James Carston paid little attention to the singing, none whatever to the prayer, though his head was bowed. He was lost in his own thoughts during the opening paragraph of the minister's talk, but was brought back by the words, "Have you seen the star? You men and women of this city . . ." and his boy's question, "Have you seen the star, Daddy?" The minister was certain that not many had seen it. He said that men today found it difficult to seek stars; they loved their own will and way, were filled with pride, were steeped in greed and selfishness . . .

James Carston walked home that night alone. Ever since the day when the court, at the bidding of his influence, his money, and his demand, had given the boy into his keeping for the half year, the holidays had been a source of dread. As the child grew older, the strange arrangement of a mother in the summer and a father in the winter, and never both, puzzled him, and of late his questions were hard to answer. Some day the boy would have to be told. What should he tell him? What would she tell him? What poor reinforcement their example would be when it was his turn to meet life's temptations.

On the way to his own room, the father stopped to look at the boy. How often he stood gazing down at the child so like himself, wishing that he might always keep him a boy of 5. Tonight he stood longer than usual, then went to bed to lie staring into the darkness, thinking of things that even his strong will could not banish. He did not know that within a half-hour's walk she was struggling to forgive him that she might see the star.

In spite of all effort now, he remembered his taunting words when the court had given him his son, remembered the intolerant fashion in which during the first years he had dismissed her as unreasonable or laughed at her judgments. She was young, she had been the only daughter, unrestrained and petted, and he had not given her a long time to learn new ways. He felt a deep sense of shame for the first time. He gave up the fight against the memories and let them come . . . the night the boy was born . . . how courageous she had been . . . He felt for a moment that he would like to go to her and say that he had been unfair, but he had never said that to anyone. . . .

He did not see the child the next morning. It was raining, and as he stepped out into the chill air, he hated the world. Business was dull for him at the holidays, and that afternoon his work was done at three o'clock. He sat looking out over the roofs of the city, thinking in spite of himself of the boy's wish that his mother come to the Christmas tree, of the sunshine hair and the stories. She would not come of course, but what should he say to the child by way of explanation? Why not send the boy to her for Christmas? The words darted into his consciousness as if they had been spoken aloud. That, he told himself, would never do, but the words of the minister the night before persistently penetrated his thinking.

It was a perfectly appointed office—his father's position, business, home, everything he had was his father's, and yet he had never measured up as a boy or as a young man to what his father expected and hoped for him. His little son had his father's ways.

He looked up at the picture of the keen, strong face of his father on his desk. Tears sprang to his eyes and, yielding to a sudden overwhelming impulse, he bowed his head upon his desk and cried aloud, "O God help me."

He sat there a long time and then the miracle came. . . . The Creator touched the soul of the man He had made and completed His creation. The words that were wrung from the awakened soul were those of a strong man yielding himself to a greater will, saying out of desperate struggle, "I will do right . . . Thy will." The strengthening presence of a brother who had been through a man's Gethsemane stole into the office on the twelfth floor so quietly that the great noisy bustling city roared on unaware.

It was after five when he left his office. He had made his plans. He would send the child to her in the morning for the holidays and the tree would follow. When the boy was told, a shout of joy filled the house. "O Daddy, Daddy, couldn't we go now?" The "we" stung the heart of the man, who could not help the jealous pang that came as the boy clapped his hands and danced around the room.

Putting the child to bed that night was a difficult task for the boy's aunt, but she made no comment. When, hours later, James Carston looked in at him, the child stirred in his sleep, opened his eyes and, seeing his father, sat up quickly and cried, "Is it morning, Daddy?" The man shook his head, kissed the sleepy little face, and told him morning would come soon, and then hurried to his own room. Despite the wakeful hours and the morning that came too quickly, the man felt a strange quietness of mind and heart that he had never known before.

At eight o'clock they telephoned to ask if Mrs.

Carston would be at home that morning. She would be there until 11. At half-past nine, his suitcase packed and dressed in the fur-trimmed coat that made him look, in his aunt's words, "perfectly adorable," the boy climbed into the motor car with his father and a maid. The man began to give instructions to the half-listening child as to what he should say and do. "Tell your mother Daddy sent you for the holidays because you wanted her at your Christmas tree. The tree will come at noon. Tell her you are a Christmas visitor. You can stay until the New Year, then Mary will come for you. Listen, sonny, be sure and telephone Daddy every day at half-past four. I'll be in the office Christmas day too. Don't forget."

The chauffeur was turning the car—there was the apartment. The man seized his son, holding him tightly, and kissed him again and again. He suddenly felt that the divine will of the heavenly court might ask him to leave with the lonely woman the child who loved her and wanted her. Somehow it seemed too much. . . .

Not until the maid picked up the suitcase did the boy realize that his father was not going in with him. He stood still on the walk. "Aren't you coming, Daddy?" and in response to his father's no, the little face shadowed. "Is it going to be like summer?" he asked sadly.

The man could hardly answer. "Run along, laddie," he said. "You're a Christmas surprise. Think how surprised she'll be. I will send the tree at noon." He watched them enter the big door of the great modern apartment, then rapidly walked away, conscious of a Presence that calmed his soul.

Alma Carston was writing a list of names when the bell rang. The day before had been the first in years that she had known peace, or even approached

happiness. The list of names included old friends whom she had long neglected, lovers of books to whom she could deliver her gifts on Christmas morning; then she planned to go to church—she had not been there on Christmas Day since she was a little girl.

With every thought of dread of the day came the soothing memory of the star that she had paid to see. Not hearing the doorbell, she was astonished to hear the exclamation of her maid and then a child's laugh. A moment later found her in the hall. The surprise was almost too much, but she heard it saying, "Daddy sent me. I'm a Christmas visitor, a surprise, and the tree will come at noon 'cause I wanted you for my Christmas tree."

Had it not been for the child's evident joy and his insistence that the suitcase be unpacked, his questions about where they should put the tree, what should be on it, whether Carl the scout might come to it—a perfect volley of questions that gave her no time to think—she could not have controlled the emotions that surged over her.

At noon, as they sat down for lunch at the little table she always used for him at the lake, he looked over at her, his face beaming, and said, "It's nice, isn't it, Mother? Just like summer, only it's almost Christmas."

She could keep back the tears no longer and fled to her room, but he followed her, calling, "Has it come? Has the tree come? Daddy said it would."

And it had. It must be attended to and there was no time for tears when a Christmas tree had to be looked after. A box filled with all sorts of decorations came with the tree and it was nearly four o'clock when tinsel and gay balls, colored chains of every sort, candles that must be lighted, Santa Clauses little and big, and a wonderful electric star were fastened to the branches to the satisfaction of both the decorators.

The child was tired and content to lie quietly in his mother's arms, listening to "The Night Before Christmas." "Tell it to me, Mother," he begged. "Daddy doesn't know it and Auntie doesn't say it like you do. . . ."

Two or three times he had said, "Is it half past four?" and as the story closed he asked again.

"Why do you want to know, darling?" she asked.

"'Cause then every day I telephone Daddy. I mustn't forget it," he answered.

"It's half past four now," she said, and he ran to the telephone. He seemed such a baby to her that she listened in astonishment as the clear little voice gave the correct number. She did not know how often he had interrupted important business interviews since he had learned the call.

"Hello, Daddy. It's come. Yes. She was very surprised. It's all decorated. Yes, it's beautiful . . . I like it . . . There aren't any presents on it but there will be in the morning . . . Yes, lots and lots." Then, in dismay she heard him pleading, "Daddy, won't you come and see it 'fore I go to bed? We can light the star when it's dark. Will you come? No, Daddy, tonight. What?"

And then he turned to his mother. "He says, 'Can he come to see it,' and I said I'd ask you. Can he, Mother? Say yes, quick. . . . You can, Daddy; I asked her nice and she says you can."

The man at the other end of the wire tried to speak calmly but the child said, "I can't hear you, Daddy—what? Then all right, good-bye. . . . He'll come at half past six," he announced. "Oh, Mother, aren't we glad."

The woman, leaning her head upon her hands, did not know what to answer. The child looked at her with misgivings as she said cheerfully, "My little boy must take a nap right away. I'll wake you at six and then we can be ready when Daddy comes."

The small arms clasped tightly about her neck, the warm kisses of the boy who from babyhood had been an unusually affectionate child, seemed so good to her after the long months that she lay beside him thinking of what it would mean if she need never let him go again. The arms relaxed and, turning on his side, the child slept quietly. She watched him pressing one soft little hand again and again to her lips. "I will tell him I have paid to see the star. I do forgive him. Do you hear me, my boy?" But the child did not hear.

She did not need to waken him, for in less than an hour he sat up, rubbing his eyes. "Has Daddy come? Can we light the star? It's dark enough, isn't it?"

He sprang out of bed to be made ready. The bell rang—it was only the last mail, very late. Again, but it was a box of flowers from a friend. Then a third time, and she heard her maid's cold and dignified greeting. The boy ran to his father but the father scarcely saw him. He looked past the child at her—the first time he had seen her for three years. There was a new wonderful light in her face. He had planned carefully what he should say to her about their being friends for the sake of the boy, but instead of the carefully chosen words he cried passionately, "Try to forgive me," and reached out both arms to her.

She looked into his face and saw there what all the years had never shown her. She did not know that he had only just found his soul, but she knew in a moment that she wanted, longed, to forgive and be forgiven. "I do, I do," she responded and went to him. Those moments seemed to blot out the pain of years.

The child stood waiting, puzzled at the scene, which did not please him. Suddenly, in a trembling voice, he protested. "Come, Mother, let's show him the tree. Daddy, just look at the star—it is lighted." But the man and woman who followed their son into the room where the tree glistened had seen another Star in whose light selfishness died, a costly star that brought reconciliation and peace, a star that all the men and women and nations of the world may see if they will pay the price.

Christmas Island

Mary Ellen Holmes

Too coincidental to be true? Yet it is true. Permission to reprint this memorable New England story came after the book manuscript had been turned in for publication. So powerful is it that we just couldn't leave it out.

Colonel Henry Gariepy, editor-in-chief of The Salvation Army's War Cry, said this about public response to the story: " 'Christmas Island' is one of the most popular articles we have ever published."

The New England villagers made it plain to Mary and Joseph Carpenter that they were not welcome. Then the miracle happened.

If you are ever lucky enough to visit Christmas Island, off the rock-bound coast of Maine, the natives will point out to you with pride and affection the home of Joseph and Mary Carpenter.

It is a tight, compact, freshly-painted little white house set in the very center of the village. Every beam and rafter, every floor board, has been laid carefully by the islanders themselves in recognition of the miracle—the miracle that, eight years ago, gave Christmas Island its name.

In the neat white house, 37-year-old Joseph Carpenter, his wife, Mary, and their 8-year-old son live happily and comfortably, at peace with each other and with the world. One large front room is a sort of Yankee traders' shop, where the villagers do a land-office business swapping everything from boats to baked goods. The islanders pay the Carpenters for the space as well as for running the shop. And so, even though Joseph is a victim of Parkinson's disease, he is independent and self-supporting.

You would never guess, watching the villagers bustling in and out day after day, that there *had* been a time—not too long ago—when everyone had signed a petition to have the Carpenters evicted.

Not from this house, mind you. They were living in the lighthouse then, and this is where the story really begins. For this is the story of the lighthouse on Gull Island, the lighthouse that gave Christmas Island its name on the twenty-fifth morning of December in 1959.

To begin, Mary and Joseph Carpenter bought the lighthouse, lock, stock, and barrel, for $460. It was hopelessly run down, a derelict tower rising sharply at the sea's edge, unpainted, weather-whipped, with a ribbon of water separating it from Gull Island. But to

the Carpenters, it was their ivory tower.

By trade, Joseph had been an automobile mechanic—a good one, with his own little shop in Portland. He was shocked to learn that September day, three months before, that he had Parkinson's disease—progressive, chronic, incurable. With their first child expected in December, they didn't know quite what to do. Joseph's limbs were already getting stiff.

Joseph's life expectancy was no doubt long, but if he were unemployable, how could he possibly plan a future for himself, for Mary, for his child? Carefully he had checked his savings, sold his shop, counted his assets. And then, almost as a godsend, he had heard about Gull Island Lighthouse. By a fluke of "horse trading" it had come into the possession of a Portland merchant who was glad to sell it. For the Carpenters it was an answer to prayer—a seeming solution to all their problems. In a small place like Gull Island, the cost of living would be less than in the city. The pace would be slower. They might even find some way to supplement their savings.

And so on the tenth of November, 1959, Joseph and Mary Carpenter came to their ivory tower.

If they had guessed how violently the villagers would react to what they termed "outsiders" taking up residence in the lighthouse, they might have hesitated. But they had no way of knowing how proud and hidebound, how steeped in tradition, the islanders were.

Their troubles began as soon as they reached the dock.

First, there was no boat for rent to ferry them across the small strip of water from the island itself to the lighthouse. Finally when Joseph, in desperation, bought one, he paid $50 for an old flat-bottom scow not worth $10.

Supplies were next, and here, too, Joseph and Mary met the undisguised resentment of the villagers. When Mary protested that the prices marked on the

shelves were much lower than the prices they had paid, the storekeeper merely grunted, "Ayeh. Not to outsiders."

From the very beginning everything went the same way. It was very clear that Gull Island wanted no part of "squatters in the lighthouse," and the sooner Joseph and Mary Carpenter headed back to the mainland, the better it would be for all concerned. Joseph would have gone back, too, many times. But for some strange reason, Mary would not leave. Especially, she would not leave after she found in the lighthouse storeroom the old driftwood cradle.

"Don't ask me to go now, Joseph," she pleaded. "I can't explain why; I don't know why. I only know that our baby *has* to be born here. Later, if you still wish it, I'll go. Oh, indeed I'll gladly go! But not yet."

So the Carpenters stayed. November lengthened into December. Joseph's disease, aggravated by the conditions around him, grew worse. His arms trembled more, and it became harder and harder for him to make the trips to the village for supplies and kerosene—especially for kerosene, for it was heavy and awkward to handle, and he could bring only a little at a time.

It seemed to Joseph that the villagers, watching him trying to haul the five-gallon cans, were just waiting for the day when he could no longer manage them at all. It was as if they were saying, "When the kerosene is gone, they'll have to move; they'll have no heat, no light, no food."

The disease would take many years to break Joseph Carpenter's body, but what the islanders did to his spirit in six short weeks was a terrible thing. And what the entire experience did to his own soul was even worse, for gradually Joseph began to hate the place, and the people, and even God Himself.

Until that Christmas morning.

There was no doctor on Gull Island. Only Joseph was with her when their son, a fine, strong, handsome manchild, was born at midnight on Christmas Eve. Only Joseph was with her to wonderingly pick up his son in his arms and to stand straight and tall—not trembling now—looking across the strip of sea to the land where they had been refused room—and kindness—and understanding.

And then a strange thing happened to Joseph. Afterward, he tried to put it into speech, but there were no words. He only knew that as he held the baby in his arms, a great joy suddenly welled up within him, and he wanted to share this supreme moment of happiness with all the world.

In that instant there was no longer any room inside him for fear of his disease or for hatred.

He turned from the bed, still holding the baby close against his chest lest his weakened hands should slip. He knew, as he looked across the strip of sea to the land beyond, that nothing mattered anymore. All the frustration and bitterness were gone, as if they never had been. Here in Joseph's arms was only hope—hope eternal, hope born in his son, just as it has been born in every child since the world began.

Gently Joseph gave the baby back to Mary and watched as she laid him in the driftwood cradle. And then, because he wanted to share this moment with the people on Gull Island, because he wanted to shout out loud to them, "Behold, my son. May he grow up a credit to your village!" because he wanted to say, "I'm not angry anymore, nor hurt or afraid. I only want to share with you this happiest moment of my life," he took from his precious store of kerosene enough fuel to fill the five huge lamps in the light-house windows.

He set them blazing, like large candles in the dark, and the five beams spread out in five directions, like the points of a giant star.

Some of the islanders saw the light. A few of them thought it might even be a distress signal, but they couldn't have cared less. And, so, unconcerned, they went about their affairs.

It was six o'clock on Christmas morning before they really found out, six o'clock when the radio commentators first began to flash across the nation the story of the miracle.

How could the villagers have guessed at exactly midnight that Mary Carpenter had given birth to her firstborn son and laid him in a driftwood cradle shaped like a manger?

And how could they have possibly known that at 10 minutes past 12, just as Joseph lit the lamps to proclaim to the world that his son had been born, the pilot of a giant airliner, lost in fog off the coast with his plane's communication system jammed, suddenly had seen the heavens open up around him and a huge five-pointed beacon shine through?

The pilot tried to explain later to the reporters in Portland what had happened but, like Joseph, he could not put it to words. All he could tell was that as the sky broke into light around him, he saw, in one horrified instant, that his plane was heading straight toward a crash landing in the center of Gull Island, with its multitude of snug little homes clustered close together; Gull Island, with its families sleeping, unaware of danger.

Sharply he veered his craft back into the upper channel of air and out to sea. Then, with the beacon to guide him, he found his course and, like a wise man led by a star, carried his 88 passengers to a three-point landing in Portland, leaving Christmas Island quietly asleep under its Christmas star.

And now you know how the island got its name, and why the villagers built the house for Joseph and Mary Carpenter. You know, too, why Christmas Island seems different from much of the rest of the world. The reason is that a spirit pervades the island—a spirit of love, understanding, and tolerance that is rare and genuine and wonderful.

It is a spirit that never can die because it is part of the miracle of Christmas, which, after all, began with the birth of a Baby and the star of forgiveness His Father lit to save our world.

The Tallest Angel

Author Unknown

Some stories are like a well-loved and mauled teddy bear—they achieve an esoteric value far above their market value. This is just such a story. It has warmed my heart—and scolded me—ever since I first heard it many years ago. It is one of those stories that surreptitiously grows on a person, preying on our subconscious and jerking us out of our smug self-righteousness.

Why? Because it hits us in one of our most vulnerable spots: how we treat the unlovely among us. Let's face it— it's as hard not to care for the beautiful ones as it is to care for the unattractive and unresponsive.

Just as we could profit from reading 1 Corinthians 13 every day of our lives, so we could from this story. Were we to do so, ours would be a more caring world.

God doesn't love me!" The words echoed sharply through the thoughts of Miss Ellis as she looked around the fourth-grade school room. Her gaze skipped lightly over the many bent heads and then rested on one in particular. "God doesn't love me!" The words had struck her mind so painfully that her mouth opened slightly in mute protest.

The child under Miss Ellis's troubled study lifted her head for a moment, scanned her classmates briefly, then bent to her book again.

Ever since the first day of school, Miss Ellis had been hurt and troubled by those bitter assertions. "God doesn't love me!" The words had come from the small 9-year-old girl who stirred again restively under the continued scrutiny of Miss Ellis. Then, bending her head to her own desk, Miss Ellis prayed in her heart for the nth time: "Help her, dear God, and help me to help her. Please show Dory that You do love her, too."

Dory sat with her geography book open upon her desk, but the thoughts that raced through her mind were not concerned with the capital of Ohio. A moment before she had felt the warm eyes of Miss Ellis upon her, and now angry sentences played tag with each other in her bowed head. Once again she heard the calm voice of Miss Ellis.

"God wants us to be happy in His love." Dory laughed bitterly to herself. How could anyone be happy with a hunched back and leg braces!

"God loves everyone," Miss Ellis had said, to which Dory had angrily replied, "But he doesn't love me—that's why He made me ugly and crippled."

"God is good."

"God is not good to me. He's mean to me, that's what, to let me grow so crooked."

Dory raised her head and looked at the children around her. Mary Ann had long golden curls; Dory had straight brown hair, pulled back tight and braided into an unlovely pigtail. Jeanetta had china-blue eyes that twinkled like evening stars; Dory had brown eyes that seemed smoky, so full of bitterness were they. Ellen Sue had a pink-rosebud mouth that readily spread into a happy smile. Well, Ellen Sue could smile. She had a lovely dimpled body and ruffled, ribboned dresses. But why should Dory smile? Her mouth was straight and tight, and her body hunched and twisted. Anyone would laugh to see ruffles on her dresses. No pink and blue dresses for her, only straight dark gowns that hung like sacks over her small hunched frame.

Suddenly hate and anger so filled the heart of the little girl that she felt she must get away from this roomful of straight-bodied children or choke. She signaled her desire to Miss Ellis, who nodded permission.

There was neither pity nor laughter in the eyes that followed Dory to the door, only casual indifference. The children had long since accepted Dory as she was. No one ever jeered at her awkwardness, nor did anyone fuss over her in pity. The children did not mean to be unkind, but knowing the limits of Dory's mobility, they usually ran off to their active games, leaving her a lonely little spectator.

Miss Ellis saw the children settle back to their studies as the door closed after Dory. She stared at the door, not seeing the door at all, only the small, hunch-backed girl.

What can I do to help her to be happy? she pondered. *What can anyone say or do to comfort and encourage such a child?*

She had talked to Dory's parents and had found them to be of little help. They seemed inclined to feel that Dory's crippled condition was a blot upon *them*, one that they did not deserve. Miss Ellis had urged them not to try to explain Dory's condition but to accept it and try to seek God's blessings through it. They were almost scornful to the idea that any blessing could be found in a crippled, unhappy child, but they did agree to come to church and to bring Dory as often as possible.

Please help Dory, prayed Miss Ellis. *Help Dory, and her parents, too.* Then the hall bell sounded, and Miss Ellis arose to dismiss her class.

The reds, yellows, and greens of autumn faded into the white of winter. The Christmas season was unfolding in the room. Tiny Christmas trees stood shyly on the window sills. A great green wreath covered the door. Its silver bells jingled whenever the door moved, and the delighted giggles of the children echoed in return. The blue-white shadows of a winter afternoon were creeping across the snow as Miss Ellis watched the excited children set up the manger scene on the low sand table.

Christmas, thought Miss Ellis, *is a time of peace and joy. Even the children feel the spirit and try to be nicer to one another.*

"Is your Christmas dress done yet, Ellen Sue?" Mary Ann asked her friend. Without waiting for an answer, she chattered on. "Mother got material for mine today—it's red, real red velvet. Oh, I can hardly wait, can you?"

"Mine is all done but the hem." Ellen Sue fairly trembled with excitement. "It's pink, with rosebuds made of ribbon."

Miss Ellis smiled, remembering the thrill of the Christmas dresses of her own girlhood. How carefully

they were planned, and how lovingly her mother had made each one. Miss Ellis leaned back to cherish the memories a moment longer. Then a movement caught her eye. Slowly, furtively, with storm-filled eyes, Dory was backing away from the chattering children. Miss Ellis' heart stirred with sympathy. She watched the unhappy child ease herself into her chair, pull a book from her desk, and bend her head over it. *She isn't studying*, thought Miss Ellis. *She is only pretending—to cover up her misery.*

Dory stared at the book in front of her, fighting against the tears that demanded release. What if one of the girls had asked her about her Christmas dress? Her Christmas dress, indeed! Would anyone call a brown sack of a dress a Christmas dress? Would the children laugh? No, Dory knew the girls wouldn't laugh. They would just feel sorry for her and her shapeless dress. Sometimes that was almost worse than if they would laugh. At least, then she would have an excuse to pour out the angry words that crowded into her throat.

"Dory," a warm voice broke in upon her thoughts. "Dory, will you help me with these Christmas decorations? You could walk along and hold them for me while I pin them up, please."

Dory arose, thankful for the diversion and thankful to be near Miss Ellis. The silver tinsel was pleasant to hold, and Miss Ellis always made her feel so much better.

Slowly they proceeded around the room, draping the tinsel garland as they went. The babble of voices in the corner by the sand table took on a new note, an insistent clamoring tone that finally burst forth in a rush of small bodies in the direction of Miss Ellis.

"Please, Miss Ellis, can I be Mary in the Christmas program?"

"Miss Ellis, I'd like to be Joseph."

"I should be Mary because I can't sing in the angel choir."

Miss Ellis raised her hand for quiet. After a moment she began: "I've already chosen the ones who will play the parts of Mary, Joseph, the shepherds, and the angel choir."

"Tell us the names; tell us the names now," the children chorused.

"All right," agreed Miss Ellis as she reached for a paper from her desk. "Here they are: Sue Ellen will be Mary; Daniel will be Joseph; John, Allen, and Morris will be the shepherds. All the rest of you will be choir angels—"

Miss Ellis scanned the eager hopeful faces around her till she saw the upturned face of Dory. There was no eager hope in her small pinched face. Dory felt from bitter experience that no one wanted a hunchback in a program. Miss Ellis could not bear the numb resignation on that small white face. Almost without realizing what she was saying, she finished the sentence. "All will be choir angels except Dory." There was a moment of hushed surprise. "Dory will be the special angel who talks to the shepherds."

All the children gasped and turned to look at Dory. Dory, a special angel? They had never thought of that. As realization penetrated Dory's amazement, a slow smile relaxed the pinched features, a little candle flame of happiness shone in the brown eyes.

Her eyes are lovely when she's happy, marveled Miss Ellis. *Oh, help her to be happy more often!*

The hall bell sounded the end of another school day, and soon all the children had bidden Miss Ellis good-bye as they hurried from the room.

All but one. All but Dory. She stood very still, as if clinging to a magic moment for as long as possible. The lights had flickered out of her eyes, and her face seemed whiter than ever before.

Miss Ellis knelt and took Dory's cold little hands in her own. "What is it, Dory? Don't you want to be a special angel, after all?"

"I do, I do—" Dory's voice broke. "But—but—I'll be a horrid, hunchbacked angel. Everyone will stare at me and laugh because angels are straight and beauti—" Dory's small body shook with uncontrollable sobs.

"Listen to me, Dory," Miss Ellis began slowly. "You are going to be my special angel. Somehow, I'm going to make you look straight and beautiful, like real angels. Will you just be happy, Dory, and let me plan it all out? Then I'll tell you all about it."

Dory lifted her head hopefully. "Do you think you can, Miss Ellis, do you think you can?"

"I know I can, Dory. Smile now, you're so pretty when you smile. And say over and over, 'God loves me, God loves me.' That will make you want to smile. Will you try it, Dory?"

A shadow of disbelief crossed Dory's face. Then she brightened with resolution.

"I'll say it, Miss Ellis, and if you can make me look

like a straight angel, I'll try to believe it."

"That's the spirit, Dory. Good-bye, now, and have nice dreams tonight."

Dory went to the door, paused a moment, then turned again to Miss Ellis.

"Yes, Dory, is there something else?"

Dory hesitated for a long moment. Then she said slowly, "Do you think I could look like a tall angel, too? I'm smaller than anyone else because my back is so bent. Do you think I could look like a tall angel?"

"I'm sure we can make you look tall," promised Miss Ellis.

Dory sighed with satisfaction and let the door swing shut behind her. The silver bells on the Christmas wreath jingled merrily, almost mockingly.

What have I done? thought Miss Ellis soberly. *I have promised a little crooked girl that she will be a tall, straight angel. I haven't the slightest idea how I am going to do it. Dear God, please help me—show me the way. For the first time since I've known her, I have seen Dory happy. Please help her to be happy in Your love, dear God. Show me the way to help her.*"

Miss Ellis went to sleep that night with the prayer still in her heart.

Morning came crisp and clear. Lacy frills of frost hung daintily from every branch and bush. Miss Ellis rubbed her eyes and looked out of her window. The sparkling white beauty of the morning reminded her of angels. Angels! She recalled her promise. She had dreamed of angels, too. What was the dream about? What was it?

Miss Ellis tapped her finger against her lip in concentration. Suddenly, as if a dark door had opened to the sunshine, the dream, the whole angel plan, swept into her mind. Idea after idea tumbled about like dancing sunbeams. She must hurry and dress; she must get to the schoolhouse early to talk to Joe, the janitor. Joe could do anything, and she was sure that Joe would help her.

At the door of the school she scarcely paused to stomp the snow from her boots. Quickly she went down to the furnace room where Joe was stoking coal into the hungry furnace.

"Joe," she began, "I need your help. I've got a big job ahead of me. I'm going to make little Dory Saunders into a tall, straight angel for our Christmas pageant."

Joe thumped his shovel down, looked at her intently, and scratched his head. "You certainly did pick yourself a job, Miss Ellis. How you going to do all this, and where do I figure?"

"It's like this, Joe." She outlined her plan to him, and Joe agreed to it.

Miss Ellis went lightly up the steps to her fourth-grade room. She greeted the children cheerily, smiling warmly at Dory. Dory returned the smile, with the candle flames of happiness glowing again in her eyes.

For Dory the day was enchanted. Round-faced angels smiled at her through the O's in her arithmetic book. The time passed dreamily on whirring angel wings. At last school was over, and she was alone with Miss Ellis, waiting to hear the marvelous plan that would make her a straight and beautiful angel.

"I've thought it all out, Dory." Miss Ellis pulled Dory close as she explained the plan. "Mrs. Brown and I are going to make you a long white gown and wings, and Joe will fix you up so you will be the tallest angel of all. But Dory, let's keep it a secret until the night of the program, shall we?"

Dory nodded vigorously. She couldn't speak. The vision was too lovely for words, so she just nodded and hugged Miss Ellis as tight as her thin arms could squeeze. Then she limped from the room.

Dory had never felt such happiness. Now she really had a place in the scheme of events. At least until Christmas, she felt, she really belonged with the other children. She was really like other children. Maybe God loved even her.

At last the night of the program came. Carols of praise to the newborn King rang through the school.

Now it was time for the Christmas pageant. Soft music invited a quiet mood, and the audience waited for the curtains to open upon a shepherd scene.

The sky was dark as the shepherds sat huddled around their fire. Then suddenly a bright light burst over the scene. The audience gasped in surprise. High up on a pedestal, dressed in a gown of shimmering white satin, Dory raised her arms in salutation.

"Fear not." Her face was radiant as she spoke. "For, behold, I bring you good tidings of great joy, which shall be to all people." Her voice gathered conviction as she continued, "For unto you is born this day in the city of David a Saviour, which is Christ the Lord."

The triumphant ring in her voice carried to the choir, and the children sang, "Glory to God in the highest, and on earth peace, good will toward men," as they had never sung before.

Dory's father blinked hard at the tears that stung his eyes, and he thought in his heart, *Why, she's a beautiful child. Why doesn't Martha curl her hair and put a ribbon in it?*

Dory's mother closed her eyes on the lovely vision, praying silently, "Forgive me, God. I haven't appreciated the good things about Dory because I've been so busy complaining about her misfortunes."

The sound of the carols sung by the choir died away, and the curtains silently closed.

Miss Ellis hurried backstage and lifted Dory from her high pedestal.

"Dory," she asked softly, "what happened? How did you feel when you were the angel? Something wonderful happened to you. I saw it in your face."

Dory hesitated, "You'll laugh—"

"Never, never, Dory, I promise!"

"Well, while I was saying the angel message, I began to feel taller and taller and real straight." She paused and looked intently at Miss Ellis.

"Go on, dear," urged Miss Ellis gently. "What else?"

"Well, I didn't feel my braces any more. And do you know what?"

"No, what? Tell me."

"Right then I knew it was true. God does love me."

"Dory, as long as you know that is true, you'll never be really unhappy again. And someday, my dear, you will stand straight and tall and beautiful among the real angels in heaven."

The Tiny Foot

Frederic Loomis

foot. Thus what follows represents, I believe, the first time the full story has been included in a Christmas collection.

The story has to do with a terrible decision Dr. Loomis was once forced to make: whether to enable a deformed fetus to be born. I strongly suspect you will be no more able to forget this story than I.

Many years ago I read the moving, true story of Dr. Loomis, a West Coast obstetrician who worked such long hours that he was becoming old before his time. A patient, observing the weariness etched into his face, was bold enough to give him a prescription, one that she had seen some time before in a Chinese garden half a world away. The prescription, "Enjoy yourself; it's later than you think," radically altered Dr. Loomis's life.

And so when, six years later, I came across another story having to do with Dr. Loomis, I read it with more than ordinary interest. I have never been able to get this story, "The Tiny Foot," out of my mind. Short as it was, there was no question but that it had to be included in this collection.

I don't believe it was mere happenstance that just recently I stumbled on Consultation Room in an old book store, hemmed in by tens of thousands of paperback books. It was written by my now old friend, Dr. Loomis. Imagine my surprise and delight to discover that one chapter of the book tells in full the larger story of the tiny

Doctor, just a moment, please, before you go into the delivery room."

The man was about 35, well dressed and intelligent, an executive of a large oil company. His first baby was to arrive within the hour. He had spent the preceding hours by his wife's bedside, miserable with the feeling of helplessness and anxiety common to all prospective fathers at such a time, but nevertheless standing by to comfort her by his presence.

"I must tell you one thing before the baby gets here, doctor," he said. "I want that baby and so does Irene, more than we ever wanted anything else, I think—but *not* if it isn't all right. I want you to promise me right now that if it is defective—and I know you can usually tell—you will not let it live. No one need ever know it, but *it must not live.* I am depending on you."

Few doctors have escaped that problem. I had not been in California long before I encountered it there, just as I had encountered it elsewhere. Fortunately, it is a problem that usually solves itself. Babies that are defective, either mentally or physically, after all are infrequent. Yet the possibility of having one hounds almost every waiting mother. Her first question on opening her eyes after a baby is born is always either "What is it?" or "Is it all right?" Whichever question comes first, the other invariably follows, and the one as to its condition is always the more important.

However they may feel about it in individual instances, doctors rightly resent and resist the rather persistent effort to make them the judges of life and death. Our load of responsibility is enough without that. "Judgment is difficult," Hippocrates said, "when the preservation of life is the only question." If the added burden of deciding whether or not life *should* be preserved were placed upon us, it would be entirely too much. Moreover, the entire morale of medicine would be immediately threatened or destroyed.

Two years after I came to California, there came to my office one day a fragile young woman, expecting her first baby. Her history was not good from an emotional standpoint, though she came from a fine family.

I built her up as well as I could and found her increasingly wholesome and interesting as time went on, partly because of the effort she was making to be calm and patient and to keep her emotional and nervous reactions under control.

One month before her baby was due, her routine examination showed that her baby was in a breech position. As a rule, the baby's head is in the lower part of the uterus for months before delivery, not because it is heavier and "sinks" in the surrounding fluid, but simply because it fits more comfortably in that position. There is no routine spontaneous "turning" of all babies at the seventh or eighth month, as is so generally supposed, but the occasional baby found in a breech position in the last month not infrequently changes to the normal vertex position with the head down by the time it is ready to be born, so that only about one baby in 25 is born in the breech position.

This is fortunate, as the death rate of breech babies is comparatively high because of the difficulty in delivering the after-coming head, and the imperative need of delivering it rather quickly after the body is born. At that moment the cord becomes compressed between the baby's hard little head and the mother's bony pelvis. When no oxygen reaches the baby's bloodstream, it inevitably dies in a few short minutes. Everyone in the delivery room is tense, except the mother herself, in a breech delivery, especially if it is a first baby, when the difficulty is greater. The mother is usually quietly asleep or almost so.

The case I was speaking of was a "complete" breech—the baby's legs and feet being folded under it, tailor-fashion—in contrast to the "frank" breech, in which the thighs and legs are folded back on a baby's body like a jackknife, the little rear end backing its way into the world first of all.

The hardest thing for the attending doctor to do

with any breech delivery is to keep his hands away from it until the natural forces of expulsion have thoroughly dilated the firm maternal structures that delay its progress. I waited as patiently as I could, sending frequent messages to the excited family in the corridor outside.

At last the time had come, and I gently drew down one little foot. I grasped the other but, for some reason I could not understand, it would not come down beside the first one. I pulled again, gently enough but with a little force, with light pressure on the abdomen from above by my assisting nurse, and the baby's body moved down just enough for me to see that it was a little girl—and then, to my consternation, I saw that the other foot would *never* be beside the first one. The entire thigh from the hip to the knee was missing and that one foot never could reach below the opposite knee. And a baby girl was to suffer this, a curious defect that I had never seen before, nor have I since!

There followed the hardest struggle I have ever had with myself. I knew what a dreadful effect it would have upon the unstable nervous system of the mother. I felt sure that the family would almost certainly impoverish itself in taking the child to every famous orthopedist in the world whose achievements might offer a ray of hope.

Most of all, I saw this little girl sitting sadly by herself while other girls laughed and danced and ran and played—and then I suddenly realized that there was something that would save every pang but one,

and that one thing was in my power.

One breech baby in 10 dies in delivery because it is not delivered rapidly enough, and now—if only I did not hurry! If I could slow my hand, if I could make myself delay those few short moments. It would not be an easy delivery, anyway. No one in all this world would ever know. The mother, after the first shock of grief, would probably be glad she had lost a child so sadly handicapped. In a year or two she would try again and this tragic fate would never be repeated.

"Don't bring this suffering upon them," the small voice within me said. "This baby has never taken a breath—don't let her ever take one. You probably can't get it out in time, anyway. *Don't hurry.* Don't be a fool and bring this terrible thing upon them. Suppose your conscience does hurt a little; can't you stand it better than they can? Maybe your conscience will hurt worse if you *do* get it out in time."

I motioned to the nurse for the warm sterile towel that is always ready for me in a breech delivery to wrap around the baby's body so that the stimulation of the cold air of the outside world may not induce a sudden expansion of the baby's chest, causing the aspiration of fluid or mucus that might bring death.

But this time the towel was only to conceal from the attending nurses that which my eyes alone had seen. With the touch of that pitiful little foot in my hand, a pang of sorrow for the baby's future swept through me, and my decision was made.

I glanced at the clock. Three of the allotted seven or eight minutes had already gone. Every eye in the room was upon me and I could feel the tension in their eagerness to do instantly what I asked, totally unaware of what I was feeling. I hoped they could not possibly detect the tension of my own struggle at that moment.

These nurses had seen me deliver dozens of breech babies successfully—yes, and they had seen me fail, too. Now they were going to see me fail again. For the first time in my medical life I was deliberately discarding what I had been taught was right for something that I felt sure was better.

I slipped my hand beneath the towel to feel the pulsations of the baby's cord, a certain index of its condition. Two or three minutes more would be enough. So that I might seem to be doing something, I drew the baby down a little lower to "split out" the arms, the usual next step, and as I did so the little pink foot on the good side bobbed out from its protecting towel and pressed firmly against my slowly moving hand, the hand into whose keeping the safety of the mother and the baby had been entrusted. There was a sudden convulsive movement of the baby's body, an

Health, Peace, and sweet content be yours.
Shakespeare

actual feeling of strength and life and vigor.

It was too much. I couldn't do it. I delivered the baby with her pitiful little leg. I told the family and the next day, with a catch in my voice, I told the mother.

Every foreboding came true. The mother was in a hospital for several months. I saw her once or twice and she looked like a wraith of her former self. I heard of them indirectly from time to time. They had been to Rochester, Minnesota. They had been to Chicago and to Boston. Finally I lost track of them altogether.

As the years went on, I blamed myself bitterly for not having had the strength to yield to my temptation.

Through the many years that I have been here, there has developed in our hospital a pretty custom of staging an elaborate Christmas party each year for the employees, the nurses, and the doctors of the staff.

There is always a beautifully decorated tree on the stage of our little auditorium. The girls spend weeks in preparation. We have so many difficult things to do during the year, so much discipline, and so many of the stern realities of life, that we have set aside this one day to touch upon the emotional and spiritual side. It is almost like going to an impressive church service, as each year we dedicate ourselves anew to the year ahead.

This past year the arrangement was somewhat changed. The tree, on one side of the stage, had been sprayed with silver paint and was hung with scores of gleaming silver and tinsel ornaments, without a trace of color anywhere and with no lights hung upon the tree itself. It shown but faintly in the dimly lighted auditorium.

Every doctor of the staff who could possibly be there was in his seat. The first rows were reserved for the nurses and in a moment the procession entered, each girl in uniform, each one crowned by her nurse's cap, her badge of office. Around their shoulders were their blue Red Cross capes, one end tossed back to show the deep red lining.

We rose as one man to do them honor, and as the last one reached her seat and we settled in our places again, the organ began the opening notes of one of the oldest of our carols.

Slowly down the middle aisle, marching from the back of the auditorium, came 20 other girls singing softly, our own nurses, in full uniform, each holding high a lighted candle, while through the auditorium floated the familiar strains of "Silent Night." We were on our feet again instantly. I could have killed anyone who spoke to me then, because I couldn't have answered, and by the time they reached their seats I couldn't see.

And then a great blue floodlight at the back was turned on very slowly, gradually covering the tree with increasing splendor: brighter and brighter, until every ornament was almost a flame. On the opposite side of the stage a curtain was slowly drawn and we saw three lovely young musicians, all in shimmering white evening gowns. They played very softly in unison with the organ—a harp, a cello, and a violin. I am quite sure I was not the only old sissy there whose eyes were filled with tears.

I have always liked the harp and I love to watch the grace of a skillful player. I was especially fascinated by this young harpist. She played extraordinarily well, as if she loved it. Her slender fingers flickered across the strings, and as the nurses sang, her face, made beautiful by a mass of auburn hair, was upturned as if the world that moment were a wonderful and holy place.

I waited, when the short program was over, to congratulate the chief nurse on the unusual effects she had arranged. And as I sat alone, there came running down the aisle a woman whom I did not know. She came to me with arms outstretched.

"Oh, you *saw* her," she cried. "You must have recognized your baby. That was my daughter who played the harp—and I saw you watching her. Don't you remember the little girl who was born with only one good leg 17 years ago? We tried everything else first, but now she has a whole artificial leg on that side—but you would never know it, would you? She can walk, she can swim, and she can almost dance.

"But, best of all, through all those years when she couldn't do those things, she learned to use her hands so wonderfully. She is going to be one of the world's great harpists. She enters the university this year at 17. She is my whole life and now she is so happy. . . . And here she is!"

As we spoke, this sweet young girl had quietly approached us, her eyes glowing, and now she stood beside me.

"This is your first doctor, my dear—our doctor," her mother said. Her voice trembled. I could see her literally swept back, as I was, through all the years of heartache to the day when I told her what she had to face. "He was the first one to tell me about you. He brought you to me."

Impulsively I took the child in my arms. Across her warm young shoulder I saw the creeping clock of the delivery room of 17 years before. I lived again those awful moments when her life was in my hand, when I had decided on deliberate infanticide.

I held her away from me and looked at her.

"You never will know, my dear," I said, "you never will know, nor will anyone else in all the world, just what tonight has meant to me. Go back to your harp for a moment, please—and play 'Silent Night' for me alone. I have a load on my shoulders that no one has ever seen, a load that only you can take away."

Her mother sat beside me and quietly took my hand as her daughter played. Perhaps she knew what was in my mind. And as the last strains of "Silent Night, Holy Night" faded again, I think I found the answer, and the comfort, I had waited for so long.

Delayed Delivery

Cathy Miller

call for extra-special stories, sent me a copy of this prize-winning entry. I telephoned the genial editor, Carol Mulligan, who in turn contacted Cathy Miller, of Sudbury, Ontario. Mrs. Miller called me, granting permission to include this moving story of a delayed gift that arrived at just the right time.

"Christmas alone"—perhaps as bleak a two-word image as exists in the English language. It is hard enough to face Christmas alone if one has become, with the passing of time, somewhat inured to the possibility. It is something else if your life partner has been taken away from you suddenly—the sweetheart who, over the years, has meshed into oneness with you. This is the sorrow America's greatest poetess, Emily Dickinson, was thinking of when she wrote,

> *The sweeping up the Heart*
> *And putting Love away*
> *We shall not want to use again*
> *Until Eternity.*

A Canadian teacher and freelance writer responded to a 1992 Christmas story contest in her area newspaper, the Northern Life. *Her story won first prize. Mrs. Maimu Veedler, of Lively, Ontario had been given a copy of* Christmas in My Heart *and, responding to my*

There had never been a winter like this. Stella watched from the haven of her armchair as gusts of snow whipped themselves into a frenzy. She feared to stand close to the window, unreasonably afraid that somehow the blizzard might be able to reach her there, sucking her, breathless, out into the chaos. The houses across the street were all but obliterated by the fury of wind-borne flakes. Absently, the elderly woman straightened the slipcovers on the arms of her chair, her eyes glued to the spectacle beyond the glass.

Dragging her gaze away from the window, she forced herself up out of her chair and waited a moment for balance to reassert itself. Straightening her back against the pain that threatened to keep her stooped, she set out determinedly for the kitchen.

In the doorway to the next room she paused, her mind blank, wondering what purpose had propelled her there. From the vent above the stove the scream of the wind threatened to funnel the afternoon storm directly down into the tiny house. Stella focused brown eyes on the stovetop clock. The three-fifteen time reminded her that she had headed in there to take something out of the freezer for her supper. Another lonely meal that she didn't feel like preparing, much less eating.

Suddenly, she grabbed the handle of the refrigerator and leaned her forehead against the cold, white surface of the door as a wave of self-pity threatened to drown her. It was too much to bear, losing her beloved Dave this summer! How was she to endure the pain, the daily nothingness? She felt the familiar ache in her throat and squeezed her eyes tightly shut to hold the tears at bay.

Stella drew herself upright and shook her head in silent chastisement. She reiterated her litany of thanks. She had her health, her tiny home, an income that would suffice for the remainder of her days. She had her books, her television programs, her needlework. There were the pleasures of her garden in the spring and summer, walks through the wilderness park at the end of her street, and the winter birds that brightened the feeders outside her kitchen picture window. Not today though, she thought ruefully, as the blizzard hurled itself against the eastern wall of the kitchen.

"Ah, Dave, I miss you so! I never minded storms when you were here." The sound of her own voice echoed hollowly in the room. She turned on the radio that stood on the counter next to a neatly descending row of wooden canisters. A sudden joyful chorus of Christmas music filled the room but it only served to deepen her loneliness.

* * * * *

Stella had been prepared for her husband's death. Since the doctor's pronouncement of terminal lung cancer, they had both faced the inevitable, striving to make the most of their remaining time together. Dave's financial affairs had always been in order. There were no new burdens in her widowed state. It was just the awful aloneness . . . the lack of purpose to her days.

They had been a childless couple. It had been their choice. Their lives had been full and rich. They had been content with busy careers, and with each other.

They had had many friends. Had. That was the operative word these days. It was bad enough losing the one person you loved with all your heart. But over the past few years, she and Dave repeatedly had to cope with the deaths of their friends and relations. They were all of an age—the age when human bodies began giving up—dying. Face it—they were old!

And now, on this first Christmas without Dave, Stella would be on her own. Mable and Jim had invited her to spend the holiday with them in Florida, but somehow that had seemed worse than staying at home alone. Not only would she miss her husband, but she would miss the snow, and the winter, and the familiarity of her home.

With shaky fingers, she lowered the volume of the radio so that the music became a muted background.

She glanced toward the fridge briefly, then decided that a hot bowl of soup would be more comforting fare this evening.

To her surprise, she saw that the mail had come. She hadn't even heard the creak of the levered mail slot in the front door. Poor mailman, out in this weather! "Neither hail, nor sleet . . ." With the inevitable wince of pain, she bent to retrieve the damp, white envelopes from the floor. Moving into the living room, she sat on the piano bench to open them. They were mostly Christmas cards, and her sad eyes smiled at the familiarity of the traditional scenes and at the loving messages inside. Carefully, her arthritic fingers arranged them among the others clustered on the piano top. In her entire house, they were the only seasonal decoration. The holiday was less than a week away, but she just did not have the heart to put up a silly tree, or even set up the stable that Dave had built with his own hands.

Suddenly engulfed by the loneliness of it all, Stella buried her lined face in her hands, lowering her elbows to the piano keys in a harsh, abrasive discord, and let the tears come. How would she possibly get through Christmas and the winter beyond it? She longed to climb into bed and bury herself in a cocoon of blankets, not emerging until her friends and spring returned.

The ring of the doorbell echoed the high-pitched, discordant piano notes and was so unexpected that Stella had to stifle a small scream of surprise. Now who could possibly be calling on her on a day like

today? Wiping her eyes, she noticed for the first time how dark the room had become. The doorbell sounded a second time.

Using the piano for leverage, she raised herself upright and headed for the front hall, switching on the living room light as she passed. She opened the wooden door and stared through the screened window of the storm door in consternation. On her front porch, buffeted by waves of wind and snow, stood a strange, young man, whose hatless head was barely visible above the large carton in his arms. She peered beyond him to the driveway, but there was nothing about the small car to give clue to his identity. Returning her gaze to him, she saw that his hands were bare and his eyebrows had lifted in an expression of hopeful appeal that was fast disappearing behind the frost forming on the glass. Summoning courage, the elderly lady opened the door slightly and he stepped sideways to speak into the space.

"Mrs. Thornhope?"

She nodded affirmation, her extended arm beginning to tremble with cold and the strain of holding the door against the wind. He continued, predictably, "I have a package for you."

Curiosity drove warning thoughts from her mind. She pushed the door far enough to enable the stranger to shoulder it and stepped back into the foyer to make room for him. He entered, bringing with him the frozen breath of the storm. Smiling, he placed his burden carefully on the floor and stood to retrieve an envelope that protruded from his pocket. As he handed it to her, a sound came from the box. Stella actually jumped. The man laughed in apology and bent to straighten up the cardboard flaps, holding them open in an invitation for her to peek inside. She advanced cautiously, then turned her gaze downward.

It was a dog! To be more exact, a golden labrador retriever puppy. As the gentleman lifted its squirming body up into his arms, he explained, "This is for you, ma'am. He's 6 weeks old and completely housebroken." The young pup wiggled in happiness at being released from captivity and thrust ecstatic, wet kisses in the direction of his benefactor's chin. "We were supposed to deliver him on Christmas Eve," he continued with some difficulty, as he strove to rescue his chin from the wet little tongue, "but the staff at the kennels start their holidays tomorrow. Hope you don't mind an early present."

Shock had stolen her ability to think clearly. Unable to form coherent sentences, she stammered, "But . . . I don't . . . I mean . . . who . . . ?"

The young fellow set the animal down on the doormat between them and then reached out a finger to tap the envelope she was still holding.

"There's a letter in there that explains everything, pretty much. The dog was bought last July while her mother was still pregnant. It was meant to be a Christmas gift. If you'll just wait a minute, there are some things in the car I'll get for you."

Before she could protest, he was gone, returning a moment later with a huge box of dog food, a leash, and a book entitled *Caring for Your Labrador Retriever*. All this time the puppy had sat quietly at her feet, panting happily as his brown eyes watched her.

Unbelievably, the stranger was turning to go. Desperation forced the words from her lips. "But who . . . who bought it?"

Pausing in the open doorway, his words almost snatched away by the wind that tousled his hair, he replied, "Your husband, ma'am." And then he was gone.

* * * * *

It was all in the letter. Forgetting the puppy entirely at this sight of the familiar handwriting, Stella had walked like a somnambulist to her chair by the window. Unaware that the little dog had followed her, she forced tear-filled eyes to read her husband's words. He had written it three weeks before his death and had left it with the kennel owners to be delivered along with the puppy as his last Christmas gift to her. It was full of love and encouragement and admonishments to be strong. He vowed that he was waiting for the day when she would join him. And he had sent her this young animal to keep her company until then.

Remembering the little creature for the first time, she was surprised to find him quietly looking up at her, his small panting mouth resembling a comic smile. Stella put the pages aside and reached down for the bundle of golden fur. She had thought that he would be heavier, but he was only the size and weight of a sofa pillow. And so soft and warm. She cradled him in her arms and he licked her jawbone, then cuddled up into the hollow of her neck. The tears began anew at this exchange of affection and the dog endured her crying without moving.

Finally, Stella lowered him to her lap, where he regarded her solemnly. She wiped vaguely at her wet cheeks, then somehow mustered a smile.

"Well, little guy, I guess it's you and me." His pink tongue panted in agreement. Stella's smile strengthened and her gaze shifted sideways to the window. Dusk had fallen, and the storm seemed to have spent the worst of its fury. Through fluffy flakes that were now drifting down at a gentler pace, she saw the cheery Christmas lights that edged the roof lines of her neighbors' homes. The strains of "Joy to the World" wafted in from the kitchen.

Suddenly Stella felt the most amazing sensation of peace and benediction washing over her. It was like being enfolded in a loving embrace. Her heart beat painfully, but it was with joy and wonder, not grief or loneliness. She need never feel alone again. Returning her attention to the dog, she spoke to him, "You know, fella, I have a box in the basement that I think you'd like. There's a tree in it and some decorations and lights that will impress you like crazy! And I think I can find that old stable down there, too. What d'ya say we go hunt it up?" The puppy barked happily in agreement, as if he understood every word.

The Locking in of Lisabeth

Temple Bailey

How impossible it is to accurately judge a person's true worth by the exterior facade! Yet we try to do it often, failing to realize that many a person barricades a soft heart behind a crusty wall. This wall may once have been so thin and fragile it could have been easily shattered, but it grows and grows till it is brick thick. The following long-loved story deals with a man who once made a foolish choice and suffered because of it for most of his adult lifetime. However, an odd incident paved his way through the self-imposed wall and into the light.

Christmas was the same as any other day to Judge Blair. He lived alone and ate his Christmas dinner alone, and never gave presents. In fact, he was like the miller of Dee: since he cared for nobody, of course, nobody cared for him.

On Christmas Eve the judge stayed late at his office. His clerks left at five.

"A Merry Christmas, Judge!" said Miss Jenkins, his stenographer, as she prepared to leave.

The judge looked up from his papers and stared at her over his glasses. "What's that? Oh, thank you, Miss Jenkins." But he did not return the greeting, and timid little Miss Jenkins blushed and wondered if she had been too bold.

At half past six a waiter from a nearby restaurant brought in a light supper. The judge often supped at his office when he had an important case on hand. It saved time.

"A Merry Christmas, suh!" said the waiter, when he had arranged the tray in front of the old gentleman.

"Hum? Oh, ah, yeah—you may call for the tray later, George," said the judge, and George departed crestfallen. If he banged the door on which was painted in imposing gilt letters MARCELLUS BLAIR, ATTORNEY AT LAW a little more vigorously than was necessary, why, who shall blame him?

The judge read over his brief while he ate, pausing now and then to pick up his lead pencil and make corrections in his neat legal hand. Suddenly he straightened up and looked around the room. "Now, what was that?" he murmured, looking over his eyeglasses.

Tap, tap, came a sound against the pane. He listened a moment and then went back to his work;

but hearing it again, he rose and went to the window and raised the shade.

There was a narrow space between the building in which the judge had his offices on the fourth floor and the big public school next to it. But the snow sifted in between, and it was very dark.

Suddenly out of the blackness came the end of a long wand, which hit the windowpane once, twice, quite sharply before the judge raised the sash with a bang. "Who's that?" he cried harshly.

"Please," said a very small voice across the way.

"Who's there?" asked the judge, peering into the darkness.

"It's me," said the little voice.

"Who's me?" demanded the judge.

"Lisabeth."

"Where are you?"

"I'm in the school room. I've tried and tried to get out, but I'm locked in; and I've been here since all the afternoon," the voice wailed. Tears were not far away.

"WHAT?" exclaimed the judge.

"Yes, sir, I came back to get my books; and the girls had all gone home, and I s'pose the janitor thought everybody was out and locked the outside door; and I banged and banged, but nobody heard me."

"Why didn't you call before?"

"I tried to, but couldn't make you hear, until I thought of the pointer."

"Well, well, well," said the judge. Then he lighted a match. "Lean out a bit and let me see you,"

he commanded. The yellow glare showed a pale little face with earnest blue eyes, red-rimmed from crying, and fair hair braided in a thick braid.

"Why haven't your people looked you up?" the old gentleman asked querulously, as the light went out.

"I haven't any people," sighed Lisabeth, "only my sister."

"How old is she?"

"Oh, she'll soon be 16, and she works at Roby's ribbon counter. She won't get home till late tonight, 'cause they don't shut up until late on Christmas Eve."

"Hum," said the judge crustily. "I suppose I'll have to look after you."

He went back to his desk, and Lisabeth, shivering at the open window, saw him pick up the telephone receiver.

Suddenly he put it down and came back to the window.

"Are you hungry?" he asked.

"Awfully," said the little voice in the darkness.

"Why didn't you say so before—" questioned the judge testily—"before I ate up my dinner?"

"I couldn't make you hear, you know," was the patient answer.

"Well, there's nothing left but some crackers and an orange."

"Oh, an orange!" Lisabeth's sigh was rapturous.

"Do you want them?"

"Oh, yes, thank you." Lisabeth wondered how the judge could ask such a question. But the judge had gone back to his desk, and was emptying the dish of crackers into a large manilla envelope. He laid the orange on top, pinned the flap, and tied a string around the whole.

"Reach over your pointer," he directed; and when Lisabeth had laid it across the chasm between the buildings, he hung the package upon it, and in another minute the little girl had drawn it over.

"Is it all right?" asked the judge, as he heard the crackle of the paper.

"Oh, yes, indeed! It is a delicious orange, perfectly delicious."

"Hm-m," said the judge again, but this time there was just a ghost of a smile on his face as he went over to the telephone, called up police headquarters, and gave a peremptory order.

"They'll be up in a minute to let you out," he informed Lisabeth as he came back to the window. "And now I've got to get back to work, and you'd better shut the window."

"It's very dark," quavered the little voice.

Somewhere back in the judge's past there had been a little child who at night would say, "It is very dark, Father; stay with me," and the judge had stayed, and had held the little clinging fingers until the child slept. But when the child grew to be a man, he had married a lady who did not please the judge, although she was sweet and good; but she was poor, and the judge was proud, and had hoped for greater things for his son. And so the son had gone away, and for years the old man had shut his heart to all tenderness; but now the little voice woke memories, so that

the judge's tone was softer when he spoke again.

"Are you afraid?"

"It's dreadful lonesome," was the wistful answer, "and it's awfully nice to have you to talk to."

"Oh, is it?" said the flattered judge. "Well, you've got to wrap up if you stand there. It's freezing cold."

"Oh, I didn't think!" Lisabeth's tone was worried. "You will take cold. Oh, please shut your window."

But this the judge refused to do. "I'll put on my overcoat and pass Miss Jenkins' sweater over to you."

So while the important case waited for review, the two shrouded figures sat at opposite windows, while between them the snow came down faster and faster. The judge's office was brilliantly lighted, and Lisabeth could see every expression of the old man's face; but the judge could see nothing of the little girl, so that her voice seemed to come from out of the night.

While they waited thus, Lisabeth told the judge about her older sister, who had taken care of them both ever since their father died, and how Lisabeth kept house when she was not at school; and, best of all, she told him that she had saved $1.25 to spend for Christmas presents, and she was going to buy a pair of gloves for sister.

"And what will you have for Christmas?" asked the judge, interested in spite of himself.

"Oh, sister'll give me something," said the child cheerfully. "Prob'ly it will be something useful. If she gives me a dress, she can't give me any toys or candy. And then, besides, she had to spend quite a bit for the dinner. Things are so 'spensive."

"You see," explained Lisabeth, "we're going to divide with the McGafneys on the top floor. They're awfully poor, and there's four children, but we're going to have pumpkin pie and lots of gravy and potatoes, so as to make enough. At first we thought we wouldn't ask them, and have enough ourselves for once; but sister decided that Christmas was the time to make other people happy, and of course it is."

"Of course," assented the judge, feeling very small indeed when he thought of his gruff reply to Miss Jenkins, and of how he had sent poor George away without even a Christmas wish.

On and on chatted the little voice in the darkness, while the judge, listening, felt the ice melt around his old heart.

"I shall have to eat my dinner all alone tomorrow," he found himself confiding, presently.

"Oh, you poor man!" cried the little girl. "Maybe we'll have enough—I'll ask my sister"—but before she could finish her invitation, a loud knock echoed through the building.

"They've come," said the judge. "Now you just sit still until they come upstairs and get you. Don't go bumping around in the dark. I'll go down and see them," and out he rushed, leaving Lisabeth to face his lighted window alone.

The police having found the janitor, the door was quickly opened; the lights soon flared in the halls, and in a minute Lisabeth was surrounded by a little crowd composed of two jolly policemen, the janitor, and a half-dozen people who had watched the opening of the door.

"You'd better take her straight to the station, Murphy," said one policeman to the other, "and they can send her home from there."

"You won't do anything of the kind," said a commanding voice; and the judge came in, panting from his climb up the steps, his shoulders powdered with snow, with all the dignity that belongs to a judge, so that the policemen at sight of him touched their caps and the stragglers looked at him respectfully.

"Order a taxi, Murphy," he said; and in less time than it takes to tell it, Lisabeth found herself on the soft cushions, with the judge beside her.

"I'll take her, Judge, if you're too busy," said Murphy, with his hand on the taxi door.

But the judge had forgotten his important case. The clinging fingers, the look in the trustful blue eyes, made his old heart leap.

"Thank you, Murphy," he said; "I'll look after her. And oh, ah—a Merry Christmas, Murphy!" and he left the officer bewildered by the unusual kindliness of his tone.

As they rolled along, he pulled out his watch. "What time did you say your sister would get home?" he said.

"Not much before 10 o'clock."

"It's only eight now," said the judge, "so I will get you something to eat. Then we will call for her."

The rest of the evening was a dream to the little girl. The wonderful dining room at the great hotel, where there were flowers and cut glass and silver on the lovely white tables, seemed just like fairyland.

When they were once more in the taxi, the judge ordered the driver to go to Roby's.

A crowd of girls streamed out from the doors of the big store as they drove up, but Lisabeth made straight for a slender figure in a thin old coat. One of the girls called out.

"Marcella, Marcella Blair, wait a minute. Here's Lisabeth!"

Within the taxi the judge sat up straight and looked out at the sound of that name. She had called her "Marcella Blair," and he was Marcellus Blair!

Before Marcella could think or understand, they were in the taxi together, the sisters and an excited old gentleman, who kept asking questions: "Who was your father? How came you to be named Marcella?"

"After my grandfather," said the dazed Marcella; "He was Marcellus Blair."

And then the judge told her joyfully that he was Marcellus Blair and her grandfather, and—well, it was all so wonderful that Lisabeth simply sat speechless, and clasped her hands very tightly, and wondered if she was dreaming.

"And I have a letter from my father to you, sir,"
explained Marcella shyly. "He tried to find you after Mother's death. But you were abroad, and then—he died—and after that I did not know what to do."

"Why didn't you hunt me up?" demanded the judge. "Why didn't you hunt me up?"

"I tried to, once," said Marcella, "but the city was so big—"

"Oh, oh," groaned the judge, "and all this time I have been so lonely!"

And then Lisabeth tucked her hand into his. "But you will never be lonely anymore, Grandfather," she said.

And he wasn't, for he took Marcella and Lisabeth home with him that very night, and the very next day the McGafneys had all of the dinner for themselves, and Marcella and Lisabeth ate in the judge's great dining room. That night, as the happy three sat in the library in front of a roaring fire, Lisabeth laid her head on her grandfather's shoulder.

"It *was* lucky I was locked in, Grandfather," she said, "or you might not have found us."

But the judge, with one arm around her waist and the other reached out to Marcella, shook his head. "Don't talk of luck, dearie," he said. "It was something more than that; it was Providence."

Christmas Magic

Author Unknown

When you really love someone your first impulse is to have a monopoly on that person's affections—especially on Christmas. But when the man of the house is a frustrated romantic who grew up in a Christmasless home, well anything is likely to happen . . . and does!

This Christmas," proclaimed McRitchie proudly, "we shall have a tree!"

He looked into the depths of a frilly basket, to meet the calm gaze of his daughter, 6 weeks old.

"Yes, old lady," he continued, "it will be *some* tree. And you shall hang up your stocking, and Mother shall hang hers, and even your broken-down old dad may take a chance that Santa will not forget him. You have a wonderful grip upon my finger, daughter. Mary," with a glance at the baby's mother, who was listening amusedly to his conversation, "isn't this baby unusually husky?"

"Of course!" laughed Mary. Then her eyes grew wistful as she rose and stood beside him. "Mac," she said, "you don't *really* mind because she's not a boy?"

McRitchie looked at her reproachfully. "My dear, this is the fourteenth time you have asked that question, and each time I have replied emphatically that I *prefer* a daughter. I *love* little girls. I like their frills and ruffles. But," McRitchie sighed, "I wish she were twins! I am 43 years old, Mary; and it takes so long to accumulate a family."

Mary rubbed her cheek against his coat sleeve. "A family of three is not so bad," she replied. "Last year there were only two of us; and we thought that was pretty good—if I remember rightly. But now, Mac, I can hardly wait for Christmas morning! I—I'm glad you want a tree. We'll get a little one and have it on the dining table."

McRitchie turned, looking down on his wife soberly. Then he exploded: "A *little* one! On the *dining* table! Well, I guess not! Mary," his voice lowered, "I—I never had a Christmas tree. When I was a little kid there was no one who cared enough to fix one for me, not in my memory, you know. All my life I have looked upon them longingly. Maybe I never quite grew up. Anyway — we're going to have a big tree. It must reach within six inches of the ceiling and have all the fixings; miles of tinsel, bushels of popcorn, dozens of lights—everything, just like the pictures you see in magazines. I brought the popcorn home tonight, and all the dinky little electric lights. I — I've just got to have it, Mary."

"Oh, Mac!" said Mary tenderly.

She was continually finding out new things about her husband that made her ache for the lonely little boy he had once been. If she had only known, she would have had a tree for him the year before — the first Christmas after they were married. But this time! Of course, it was absurd to have a great big tree for a baby who would only blink at it; but it was not absurd to have a tree for Mac! It should be the tree of his dreams, to every minutest detail. Mary caught his hand and squeezed it.

"Mac, I'd love it! I have not had a tree for years and years. It'll be a real family Christmas this year— just for the three of us. Oh, Mac! Isn't it great to be a family at Christmas time?"

There followed busy and exciting days. As the time passed, Mary wondered if her husband spent his entire noon hour in an orgy of shopping at the 10 cent store. Each night he appeared with some new trinkets, which he opened mysteriously and held proudly before Mary's eyes.

These treasures he hid carefully on the top shelf of the china closet, as if he feared the baby might get an untimely glimpse of them. For the first time in his life McRitchie was reveling in the mysteries of Christmas.

But the most important purchases were made the day Mary went to town. Mrs. Fisher, whose husband worked under McRitchie at the office, and who owed the older man a debt of gratitude, appeared bright and early to care for the baby in Mary's absence. She brought her own baby, a year old and "a perfect darling," cried Mary, as the child laughed and held up her little arms.

"I won't be gone long, Mrs. Fisher, and baby will sleep most of the time. If you're hungry there's sponge cake in the box, and we'll have luncheon when I get back."

"Now don't you hurry," said Mrs. Fisher, cheerfully. "I love it here. It's a treat to have a change." She glanced about. "Somehow I can't make my house look just like yours," she added wistfully.

Mary smiled. "But you would not want it to look *just* like mine," she answered. "Houses should look like the people who live in them, you know. Your house is lovely, Mrs. Fisher, especially since you got that pretty paper for your living room."

"You didn't mind my getting it like yours?" asked the girl shyly.

"Indeed, no!" cried Mary. "I felt quite flattered. Now, I must go. Just look outside and see the Christmas tree. Mac's going to set it up tonight."

She stopped to drop a kiss on the girl's cheek. It was a cheek that six months before had held a touch of rouge. It didn't need rouge now, thought Mary, as she walked briskly toward the station. Country air had whipped color into the pale face; and there were other changes. In her mind Mary compared the trim serge dress Mrs. Fisher wore today with the flimsy, transparent shirtwaist she would have worn before, and smiled tenderly at the girl's efforts to copy everything she did herself.

She was a nice little thing, thought Mary. It was a pity Fisher's sisters considered her beneath their notice. But it was really hardest on the sisters. They had no one but Fisher; and Mrs. Fisher had her husband and the baby, too. A baby was so adorable at Christmas, thought Mary happily; and it would be a glorious Christmas this year: a long blissful day with just Mac and the baby. For once, McRitchie hadn't suggested inviting anybody else.

This last fact Mary hugged jealously to herself. Mac was so dear. He always wanted to share everything he had with everybody who hadn't quite so much, especially the people in the office, whose happiness he considered his special care. But on Christmas it *was* nice to be alone.

One by one Mary had entertained the whole office force, from Mr. Corey, the mummified head of the firm, to Thomas, the elevator boy. Mary herself had worked in the same office before their marriage, so most of their guests, including Thomas, were old friends. There were new ones now in some of the departments. And Mary's own desk was occupied by Fisher's younger sister. She had recently lost money, and Fisher had asked Mac to take her on, in spite of the coolness between himself and his family, who had never failed to show their disapproval of his marriage.

She did her work, Mac said, as if she were conferring a favor upon the firm; but it was work she needed, which was the main thing, he added, with true McRitchie reasoning. It hurt McRitchie a little that Fisher rarely spoke to his sister in the office.

"Not that I really blame him," he said to Mary, "after the snippy way she treats his wife, and taking no notice whatever of the baby."

McRitchie met her at the station, and together they finished the purchases for the tree. Her husband was like a boy, hesitating over each shining ornament as if the fate of a nation rested between a sparkling icicle and a Christmas rose. He ended by purchasing a wonderful Christmas star for the top of the tree, and a red-clothed Santa Claus for the baby.

"Now, don't you dare get anything for me!" she scolded.

"All right," said McRitchie grinning joyfully. "I won't bother about you. Of course, being the whole show myself, it doesn't matter whether any one remembers you or not. Say, I've got to get back to the office now. Do you think the crowd would notice if I kissed you?"

"Yes, I do," laughed Mary. "Don't you dare!"

McRitchie was rather quiet that night at supper, but his spirits rose during the process of putting the tree up. It *was* a lovely tree, tall and symmetrical as one could wish, reaching, as Mac had stipulated, just six inches from the ceiling.

"I'm dying to trim it, Mary" he said boyishly. "Can't I put a few things on and take 'em off again?"

"No," Mary replied severely. "You must string the popcorn. And why you bought all those cornucopias for candy, when there is no one to eat it but you and me—"

"But—but they always have 'em on Christmas trees in pictures," began McRitchie uneasily. "And —well, it's a pretty big tree for just one little baby, Mary."

"It isn't just for a baby," said Mary gently. "It's for a little boy who never had a Christmas tree years ago. As for the cornucopias—" She stopped abruptly as a sudden suspicion of truth flashed into her mind. "Mac—it isn't possible—"

The dreadful certainty that was creeping over Mary was confirmed by the guilty look in her husband's face. For a moment she could not find her voice, and McRitchie also became strangely dumb. It was the most uncomfortable moment of their married life. Then Mary's sense of humor came to the rescue, and she said shakily:

"You might as well confess, Mac. How many people have you invited for Christmas dinner?"

His face brightened suddenly, like sunshine.

"Not one! On my honor, Mary, not one! Do you think I am such a beast as to ask you to get dinner for a crowd, when you haven't half your strength back? But I thought in—in the afternoon, you know— some of 'em might like to see the tree and—and— the baby. We could have some hot chocolate, maybe. I'll make it, Mary, and wash all the dishes. You see, dear, that little Miss Spencer from Vermont is homesick. I

caught her crying the other day; and before I thought what I was up to, I asked her to come out Christmas afternoon. I—I think she's had a quarrel with Billy Hall, the bookkeeper. I asked him, too. I thought maybe they'd make up on the train, or something. And then—"

"Yes?" said Mary as he hesitated.

"Well," plunged McRitchie desperately, "there's Miss Knowlton. It's the first Christmas without her mother. She was wild to come. And Mrs. Thompson's just back from the sanitarium and I thought that if—if they dropped in a while it would do her good. The boy would love the tree, Mary, and we could have a package for him. The Taylors can't come because they're going to her mother's; but Thomas almost shot the elevator through the roof, he was so pleased when I asked him. And Mr. Corey—"

"*Mr. Corey!*" exploded Mary. "You do not mean you asked Mr. Corey, Mac? To our little house—on Christmas?"

"Why not?" answered McRitchie innocently. "I —I'm sorrier for him than for anybody! Living with a tragedy, the way he does. Why, he just ate the invitation right up, Mary. He said Christmas was the hardest day in the whole year."

"Did—did you ask the janitor?" asked Mary weakly.

"Of course," Mac answered soberly, "but he said he always spent the day with his in-laws." McRitchie's eyes twinkled. "He did not seem very enthusiastic about in-law Christmases, either. But the Fishers will come, and—oh, look here! are you awfully disappointed, darling? If you only knew—"

"Knew what?" asked Mary, hoping her consternation was absent from her voice.

"How—how awfully lonesome a lonesome Christmas is, dear. Do you know, all those years I lived in a hall bedroom no one ever asked me to a Christmas dinner, or to have a glimpse of a tree, or—or anything. I suppose because I did not talk about it they thought I had somewhere to go. Once I spent the whole day in the office. It was more like home than any place I knew. Sometimes I wandered around the streets at night, hoping someone would leave a shade up so I could steal a look at all the fun. And now when I have so much, Mary; you and the baby—and a *home—*!"

McRitchie swallowed something as he felt Mary's warm cheek against his own.

"It will be splendid!" she said generously. "I'll ask Mrs. Fisher to help me make some doughnuts. No one will want much supper Christmas night. And there should be a little package for everybody on the tree, jokes—or something to make them laugh. I guess you'll have to do some more shopping, Mac. I can't get to town again to save my life. We'll make a list now and plan everything. We can sing carols, and we'll borrow the Fisher's phonograph and have a Virginia reel. It's lucky we made these two rooms into one. I shan't sleep a wink tonight, I'm so excited."

"Are you?" cried McRitchie happily. "You know I was sort of afraid you might be disappointed—or something."

If Mary was disappointed she disguised it well, yet there were moments when it vaguely hurt her to think that Mac had asked outsiders on their first Christmas with their baby, well as she understood his impulsive generosity. But these moments were few and far between. This was Mac's first Christmas tree, and she was determined to make it a success. On Christmas Eve, when the last shining bauble was in place, they fairly hugged each other in delight.

"And now," said Mary, "we must be sure we've forgotten no one. Here's the list of names, Mac, and what we've got for them. I couldn't contrive jokes for everyone, but there are enough to make some fun. I haven't forgotten anybody, have I?"

McRitchie took the list, smiling delightedly as he read Mary's jokes. Then suddenly, he exclaimed, "Good land, Mary! I 'most forgot to tell you! I invited Fisher's sisters."

Mary stared. "But—but what shall we do? They hardly speak to Mrs. Fisher, and—"

"I had to, Mary, truly," explained McRitchie. "When I got into the outer hall tonight one of 'em was waiting for me—the one with the long nose."

Mary giggled, and McRitchie added: "You needn't laugh. It's awfully long and pointed. It always seems to get there ahead of her. Well, I saw she wanted to say something, and after a lot of beating about the bush, she lugged out a package done up in ribbons and tissue paper. She asked if I would leave it at her brother's on my way home. It was for the baby."

"Mercy!" gasped Mary in surprise.

"That was what I thought," said McRitchie. "She did not tell her sister—the one that works in the office, you know. And just then that one burst out of the door and I tucked the package under my coat. Sister had evidently been crying, and Fisher was just behind her. He started when he saw who was talking with me, and nodded like an icicle and went downstairs. He did not wait for the elevator. I wanted to punch him; but I was sorry for him, too. *He* didn't know about the package. And he loves that little wife of his a good sight more than he did before he married her. But—those girls looked kind of pitiful to me. They're older than Fisher, and they adore him. So— well, I invited them; and they jumped at the chance. I guess they were feeling lonely. Can't you scare up something to give 'em, honey?"

"I may have some new handkerchiefs," said Mary dazedly.

"That'll do for Caroline," said McRitchie, "but I shouldn't want to give anything to Lydia that might draw attention to her nose."

His kindly meaning was so genuine that Mary rocked with mirth.

"A sachet would be almost worse," she laughed. "Well—I've a new crepe tie I'll sacrifice, though I had planned to wear it. Oh, Mac, you are the funniest! I only hope your impulsive invitations won't spoil the party."

"It can't—on *Christmas*," replied McRitchie optimistically. "Come, Mary, let's fill the stockings and go to bed. I'll never forgive myself if you get tired. My dear — I'm afraid your stocking will be pretty empty."

The sparkle in his eyes belied his words, and Mary smiled.

"Don't worry. There won't be much in yours. We'll fill baby's first. Doesn't it look darling, Mac, hanging there between our two big ones?"

McRitchie lifted the tiny pink silk stocking tenderly. "To think, Mary, that such a thing belongs to *us*! It seems incredible. This—won't hold much, honey."

"It'll hold this rubber doll and worsted ball. Somehow, I don't think Miss McRitchie will know the difference."

"And I've got two little candy canes. We'll put those in for looks. There, Mary! Who dares tell me that dreams don't come true."

"Not I," said Mary, as McRitchie kissed her.

"Now shall I fill your stocking while you turn your back, or—"

"You'll fill it while I fix the furnace, and then you'll scoot upstairs. This is a new job to me. I want the whole place to myself. Do you know, Mary, I feel just like a kid."

"You won't peek at things when I'm gone then?" asked Mary sternly.

"Cross my heart," laughed Mac as he descended cellarward.

It was a glorious Christmas morning. A snowstorm the night before had frosted everything. Miss

McRitchie awoke her parents with a demand for breakfast, and then seconds later her dad was wishing her a Merry Christmas.

Afterward (he hadn't allowed Mary even to start the coffee) they sat on the floor before the fireplace, and baby cuddled in her father's arms.

"Don't try to tell me this kid's too young to enjoy Christmas!" exclaimed McRitchie. "She's trying to eat up all her presents."

"If you let her eat those candy canes you may regret it," replied the baby's mother. "Open your stocking, Mac, I can't wait another moment to look at mine. There's only one thing in yours, except the oranges to make it bulky, so don't be disappointed."

"And there's *nothing* in yours except the bulky thing. Your present's in that box beside the fender . . . Oh, Mary! The idea of your getting me those fur-lined gloves! Is it possible my thrifty wife is turning out a spendthrift! I love 'em, dear. Come nearer so I can hug you."

"Wait!" said Mary. She was untying her box as excitedly as a child. "Oh, Mac! Mac!" Her eyes swam with tears as she buried her face in the soft furs—furs she had wanted for so long. "Don't you talk about extravagance," she said shakily. "I know now why you would not get an overcoat. And your old one's so —so shabby—"

"It is *not*. And even if it were, think how the other men will envy me my stunning wife. Put 'em on, dear—quick! Are they what you want? You can change them if —"

"Change them!" echoed Mary indignantly. "Mac, I feel like a duchess. I shall want to wear them every minute! I shall go to *bed* in them! Oh, Mac!"

* * * * *

The first of the McRitchie guests to arrive were the Fishers, at three o'clock, armed with a baby, a blossoming azalea plant for Mary, and what McRitchie called a "monument of doughnuts," since Mrs. Fisher had insisted on making every one. Mary had made sugar cookies and gingerbread; a huge caldron of chocolate was on the stove, and there was grape juice and lemonade for those who wanted to cool off. Mary, seeing the Fishers turn in at the gate, hoped devoutly that Fisher's sisters would be the last arrivals. In a crowd things would be less awkward.

"Merry Christmas!" welcomed McRitchie, throwing wide the door. "Fisher, you dump those doughnuts in the kitchen. Mary's upstairs, Mrs. Fisher. I believe she wants you. She's going to rope you into pouring chocolate when the guests arrive."

This had been an inspiration on Mary's part. She was going to show those haughty sisters that Mrs. Fisher could do things gracefully. She had telephoned that morning to ask as a favor that Mrs. Fisher wear her dark blue taffeta. It was her most becoming dress, and Mary was bound she look her best.

"Come up!" she called over the banister. "Baby's asleep. I hope she will sleep an hour longer, for Mac's sure to keep her up outrageously. I know her habits will be in ruins by night; but we can't help it. Christmas comes but once a year and—oh, Mrs. Fisher, how sweet your baby looks in that little jacket! And her hair is curling! I told you it would curl. Oh, I wish the Taylors were coming with all their children! This is an awfully grown-up Christmas party; just your baby and ours, and little Harold Thompson. Thomas is only 14, but I suppose he'd resent being called a child."

"Mr. Fisher's sister Lydia made the little jacket," said Mrs. Fisher proudly, "and Caroline sent that cunning pin. She gave it to Mr. Fisher in the office. I thought I would let her wear them both. It—it made Mr. Fisher so happy to have them do it."

"Of course it did!" said Mary gently. "Here—let me carry the baby down for you. I can't keep away from her, she looks so dear."

Inwardly Mary was exulting. Fisher's sisters could *not* resist that baby! For the first time she felt glad of Mac's impulsive invitation.

"Merry Christmas, Mrs. McRitchie!" cried Fisher, joyously. "Say, that's some tree! And look, honey [turning to his wife], at that little stocking. Mac left it up for the crowd to see."

Mary smiled. "It broke his heart to take it down this morning, so I told him to leave it there, though it looks rather limp without the dolly. Open the door, Mac, here comes Miss Knowlton and the Thompsons; and—yes, there's Mr. Corey's car! He's got Thomas with him and Miss Spencer and Billy Hall. He must have picked them up on the way. And—why, Mac! There *are* the Taylors! Every one of them! Isn't that too good to be true? And—and—"

Mary did not mention the last two figures turning

in at the gate. She was dimly conscious that Mrs. Fisher had darted toward the kitchen with her baby; but amid all the confusion she saw with joy that Fisher went forward and kissed both his sisters, and she knew suddenly that everything would be all right.

"I don't know what you will think of us," Mrs. Taylor was explaining breathlessly, "to say we were not coming, and then to *come!* But Mother was really too sick to have us; just a grippy cold, but she was afraid we'd all take it. So after dinner George said to come along, he knew the McRitchies wouldn't care. We tried to telephone but the wires were down. The children were crazy to see the baby, and —"

"Oh, I'm so glad!" said Mary. "The one thing this party lacked was children. Merry Christmas, Thomas! You know where to find the gingerbread. Hello, Miss Knowlton! I'll kiss you when I get near enough. Merry Christmas, Miss Spencer! You don't know how glad we are to see you! And this is Billy Hall, of course. You see, I have heard about you even if we have never met. And you two are Mr. Fisher's sisters. It's splendid that you could come. Mr. Fisher, will you find your wife and ask her to look after things while I show these people where to leave their wraps? Merry Christmas, Mr. Corey! Can you steer a double-runner? Those who want to coast may keep their things on, then the rest of you may come upstairs."

Two hours later, when the coasting party was over and the whole crowd had made the acquaintance of Miss McRitchie, Mac turned on the lights and proudly displayed the tree.

"There's not a thing on it for any of you Taylors," mourned Mary, "but there's popcorn galore, and candy —"

"Don't you worry," said Mrs. Taylor cheerfully. "The children have had one tree already, and Junior does not want anything but three bright pennies that were in his stocking. He's been hanging onto them all day. I believe he thinks they're *gold.* As for George and me —"

"Mary," interrupted Mac, "where's some tissue paper? I've a present for Taylor and nothing to do it up in."

"You see!" laughed Mrs. Taylor. "Junior!"—with a dash for her youngest — "don't tear the popcorn off the tree. It's for decoration."

"No, it isn't," contradicted McRitchie. "You can have a whole string in a minute, Sonny. Thanks, Mary. Is everybody here? We might as well distribute these costly gifts."

"Present," called Fisher from the corner. "Fire ahead, Mac."

Yes, everyone was there, thought Mary, as she looked around on the group. In Mac's big chair was Lydia Fisher, the Fisher baby on her lap. Fisher, himself, was sitting between his wife and his younger sister, brazenly holding a hand of each, and looking, somehow, more manly than of old. Mac had been right when he urged Fisher to buy a place in the country and settle down. Responsibility, and perhaps the trouble he had been through, were obliterating the weak lines about his mouth. Billy Hall stood where he could just look down upon Miss Spencer's smooth brown hair, without appearing to; and Mr. Corey was holding Mary's baby with all the ease of a veteran grandfather. The three Thompsons sat very close together on the davenport, as if they could bear no further separation after the year Mrs. Thompson had spent in a sanitarium. Miss Knowlton's plain, good-natured face was wreathed in smiles, and Thomas-of-the-elevator was fairly beaming. It was a happy crowd, thought Mary, as she sat down on the floor among the four young Taylors.

The fun began when McRitchie presented Taylor with a pencil attached to a phenomenally long string. This brought laughter, because Taylor was always losing his pencil in the office and borrowing one. Thomas blushed with pleasure and embarrassment at the gift of a safety razor, while Fisher immediately offered to show him how to use it. Miss Knowlton received a cake of scented soap, because she was constantly regretting the lack of that article in the office coatroom. And Mr. Corey, who was an inveterate smoker, but who always advised everybody else to leave the weed alone, was presented with a box of chocolate cigars, marked "Warranted harmless."

But it was Fisher, who after the gifts were all distributed, brought down the house by presenting McRitchie with a beribboned package which proved to be a copy of "How to be Happy Though Married." Everyone shouted, and there was renewed rejoicing when Mac declared he didn't need it, and passed it on to Billy Hall, which for some obscure reason brought the color to Miss Spencer's face.

Afterward, Mrs. Fisher presided at the chocolate pot, and everybody squeezed into the dining room; that is, everyone but Mr. Corey. Miss McRitchie had dropped asleep in Mr. Corey's arms, so he refused to move; and Mary, seeing that her baby was filling a long-felt want, did not insist. Later, Jerry Thompson, who could really sing, started some carols that everybody knew, and they all joined in. But the crowning fun of the day was the Virginia reel. None knew that it was a whispered word from Mary that caused Mr. Corey to invite Mrs. Fisher to head the reel with him. Mary herself was at the other end with Thomas, whose past life had not included dancing, but whose Irish feet and wit were to cause him no uneasiness.

It was a glorious reel. Everyone danced but Fisher's sister, Lydia, who refused to lay down her precious burden to join the fun. Then came a stampede for lemonade; and when every tumbler and teacup in the house was filled, it was Mr. Corey who raised his glass (it was a jelly tumbler!) and cried: "Here's to the McRitchies—God bless 'em." The cheer that followed threatened to wake the sleeping babies.

* * * * *

They were alone at last—the McRitchies. They stood looking down upon their daughter, slumbering sweetly in a corner of the davenport, unmindful that her first party was just over.

"It was a wonderful Christmas tree, daughter," said McRitchie, "and I was proud of you. I only hope that Mother is not all worn out."

"I'm not," said Mary. "And even if I were, Mac, I should not care, after seeing Mrs. Fisher's face when Fisher told her that his sisters would spend the night in her little guest room. *That* wouldn't have happened if we had not had the party."

"And when I opened the door, Mary, and discovered Billy Hall with his arms around the little Spencer girl—"

"You did?" cried Mary.

"I tried to vanish gracefully, but it was too late. Miss Spencer was the color of the red, red rose, my dear, but Billy was very bold. He said, 'Close the door, please.' "

"That's lovely," said Mary. "Mac, dear, we must go up to bed. Take down the baby's stocking and— why, look! There's something in it! It's stuffed full!"

"And heavy!" exclaimed McRitchie, lifting it wonderingly. "And here's a card. Come here on my knee, Mary, and see what's up. That's Mr. Corey's writing. It says"— McRitchie caught his breath— "it says, 'A nest egg for little Miss McRitchie, from the derelicts and others to whom her parents have given a happy Christmas.' "

Mac looked speechlessly at Mary as he emptied the little stocking into her lap. Quarters, dimes, gold pieces, three bank notes, even Junior Taylor's precious Christmas pennies, were among the hoard. The McRitchies were still dumb. Then Mac unwrapped a scrap of paper, revealing another gold piece and a penciled scrawl.

"Mr. McRitchie, I want to give this to your baby. It's the best I have. Mr. Corey gave it to me today, but I haven't any use for it, truly. I never had a family, and no one ever asked me anywhere but you. I didn't know there was such things as Christmases like this. Yours truly, Thomas."

"Oh, dear!" said Mary, chokingly. "Oh, *dear!*"

"For five cents," said McRitchie, huskily, "I could weep. This is a real nest egg, Mary. We'll add to it every year, and when that sleepyhead is ready to go to college—"

McRitchie stopped abruptly, and became absorbed in the treasure on Mary's lap.

"Mr. Corey must have given the gold pieces," he said slowly; "but whoever gave those bank notes couldn't afford it. I bet one was from Miss Knowlton —but— we'll never know. Maybe that's the beauty of it, dear. And that poor kid, Thomas—"

McRitchie's glasses suddenly needed wiping, and there came a silence before Mary spoke.

"Well, dear," she said, "I think it is up to us to see that Thomas makes something of his life. He shan't spend all of his days taking people from the first floor to the tenth of the Corey Building. We'll manage somehow to give that boy a chance.

"Oh, Mac, what a dear world it is! So full of lovely opportunities to lend a hand! When I look at that little stocking and think what it meant to some of them to be so generous, I'm just ashamed. I—I wish I were more like you, Mac. I've been so selfish. I wanted dreadfully to have the day alone with you and the baby. And now—"

"You dear goose!" cried McRitchie tenderly, "don't you know that's what I wanted, too?"

And those words were all that Mary needed to make her Christmas the perfect day.

A Father for Christmas

Author Unknown

Better than any other tale I know, this old story hammers home a great truth: the line of demarcation between success and failure in life is paper thin, as thin as the line between happiness and tragedy. Quite often the difference is nothing more than a kind heart and a realization that each of us is our brother's keeper.

Sheriff John Charles Olsen let out a sigh so hefty it blew an apple core clear off his desk. There'd been times in his life when he'd felt worse. The night he'd spent in the swamp behind the Sundquist place with a broken leg and about a million mosquitoes for company was one such time. But there'd never been a time when he'd wanted less to be a sheriff.

"Are you deaf?" Mart Dahlberg demanded.

Sheriff Olsen looked across at where his deputy was typing out letters in his usual neat and fast way. "Did you say something?"

"Only three times. Didn't you promise the fellow you'd be out there by noon?"

"It ain't noon yet."

"It will be by the time you get there."

Sheriff Olsen hauled himself, slow and heavy, to his feet.

"Sure you don't want me to go along?" Mart asked, and his voice was gentler sounding.

The sheriff shook his head. "No, not much stuff out there. Just four chairs and a table and the kids' clothes and some bedding."

"Well, I wish you'd get started," Mart said. "You got to be back here and into your Santa Claus outfit by three, remember."

"I haven't forgotten," the sheriff answered. He sounded snappish, but he couldn't help it.

Mart got up from his desk. "Look, John," he said, "take it easy. Folks get evicted from their homes all the time."

"Not a week before Christmas, they don't," the sheriff growled.

He slammed shut the office door and went out of the courthouse to where his car was parked. He gave a quick look at how the trailer was fastened, then he got into the car and slammed that door shut, too.

Maybe it wasn't anybody's fault what had happened. But it made the sheriff feel awfully queer in his stomach to have to move three little kids out of their home just before he was going to dress up in a Santa

95

Claus outfit and hand out gifts to other kids at the annual Christmas celebration!

Sheriff Olsen started up the engine and turned on the heater. Then he turned it off and wiped the sweat off his forehead with his mitten. Likely a man with more brains than the sheriff had could have fixed things right for Stephen Reade.

Sam Merske called Stephen Reade a deadbeat and a phony, but that was because Reade hadn't made a good tenant farmer. Two years ago, when Reade had rented the farm from Merske, Merske had called Reade a fine, upstanding personality.

Sheriff Olsen had argued for months with Merske about Reade and the kids, figuring that all Reade needed was another summer to get things going right. But Sam Merske was a businessman and he expected his farm to produce and make money for him. Finally he'd taken Reade to court.

After that, the sheriff had done his arguing with Judge Martinson, but the judge said that Sam Merske had been very generous and patient with Reade, and that it was understandable Sam's wanting to get a competent man settled on his farm before spring came.

"This man, Reade," the judge had said, "is obviously not fitted to farm. That has been proven to my satisfaction, not only by his inability to make his rent payments but also by the condition the county agent tells me the farm is in. Let us not fog our judgment, John, with undue sentimentality. It will be far better for both Reade and his children if we face the issue squarely."

It wasn't Stephen Reade's fault what had happened. You have to be kind of raised to it to know what to do when your cow takes sick or the weather mildews your raspberries. All his life since he was a kid, Reade had been in the selling business in New York City, going from door to door, first with magazine subscriptions, and then with stockings, and finally with vacuum cleaners. It took hard work and brains and a lot more courage than the sheriff himself had to go around ringing doorbells and asking strange women to buy things from you. But Stephen Reade had sold enough to support a wife and three children.

After the third child was born, Mrs. Reade had been sick all the time. She'd been raised on a farm in Oregon, and she figured living in a big city was what made her sick. So when she knew she wasn't going to live, she'd made her husband promise he'd take the kids to the country.

Reade had promised faithfully, and after his wife was gone he'd taken what was left of their savings and headed for Oregon. He'd gone as far as the bus depot in St. Paul when he'd read an ad. The ad had said that anyone with initiative and enterprise wanting to rent an A-one farm should apply to Sam Merske, proprietor of the Merske Dry Goods Store in Minnewashta County.

Sam had demanded three months' rent in advance, and that was all he'd ever gotten out of Reade. The cow and the chickens had taken all the leftover cash that Reade had, and the cow hadn't lived very long.

Johanna Olsen, the sheriff's wife, had bought all

her eggs off of Reade for two months. After that, for another two months she'd bought as many as Reade had to sell. And, after that, there weren't enough hens left to give the Reade youngsters an egg each for their breakfasts.

The plan was to move the Reade family into the two empty rooms above the Hovander Grain and Feed Store. It wasn't a permanent arrangement, because Hovander didn't like the idea. "Eight days is all they can stay. I ain't no charitable institution, and I wouldn't do the favor for nobody but you, John."

But the eight days would get the Reade kids through Christmas.

Sheriff Olsen brought the car and the trailer up alongside the farmhouse. There was a big railed-in porch running around three sides of the house and you could see how a widower with three children would have liked the looks of the porch the minute he saw it—forgetting how hard a big old house was to heat.

The sheriff knocked at the door. After a minute he heard someone running and then Ellen's voice said, "Robbie, don't go near that door; I'm supposed to answer." In another minute, the door opened a crack.

Sheriff Olsen said, " 'Lo, Ellen."

Ellen said, "Hello, Mr. Olsen," but she didn't smile back. "My father's out for the present, but you're welcome to wait in the kitchen. It's warmest there."

Sheriff Olsen sat down on one of the four chairs pulled up to a card table. On the table was a bundle tied up in a blanket; near the back door was a barrel covered with newspapers, and three suitcases fastened with ropes.

The sheriff said, "You sure been busy."

"I helped with everything," Robbie said.

Ellen said, "The stove belongs to Mr. Merske, and so do the beds and the clock. But the chairs and the table are all paid for and so they belong to us."

Sheriff Olsen looked at the clock. "Did your pa say when he'd be back?"

"He's gone for something," Ellen said.

Robbie said, "Dad's gone to get us a surprise. Letty thinks he's buying her a doll, but Dad said what he's getting for us is heaps more important than anything you can buy in a store."

Sheriff Olsen smiled at Letty and she came over and put her head down on his knee. She was about 4 and she wasn't worried yet about how things were in the world.

When it got to be about half past 12, the sheriff said, "Maybe we should all drive down the road a ways and give a lift to your pa!"

Ellen slid down from the window sill. "Are you getting restless, Mr. Olsen?" she asked.

"Kinda."

"Well, when you get awful restless, I'm supposed to give you a letter." She started toward the parlor door. Then she turned. "But first, you have to be awful restless."

"I am awful restless," he answered with a worried look on his kind face.

In half a minute, she was back with an envelope. Inside was a sheet of paper that had been written on with pencil:

"To the Sheriff of Minnewashta County: I, Stephen Reade, being of sound mind and body, do herewith declare that I relinquish all legal claim to my three children, Ellen, Robert, and Letitia Reade. I do this as my Christmas gift to them, so that they may be legally adopted by some family that will take care of them. I herewith swear never to make myself known to their new parents. They are good children and will make their new parents happy.

Yours very truly,

Your grateful friend, Stephen Reade."

"Does it tell about my doll?" Letty asked, jumping up and down.

"Does my father say when he'll be back, Mr. Olsen?" Ellen asked. She was standing very straight at the sink, making little pleats in her dress. "Does he?"

Sheriff Olsen looked at the clock, and then at his watch. There'd be a freight train pulling out of the station in 38 minutes, and if Reade hadn't hitched a ride on a truck, he'd be waiting to bum one on the freight. But you couldn't chase after a deserting father with the fellow's kids in the back of your car.

"Does he?" Ellen asked again.

Sheriff Olsen gave a big hearty smile. "Well, what do you know about that? Your dad's changed his plans. He wants you should stay the afternoon with my wife. So, quick now, put on your coats and caps

and boots while I unhitch the trailer."

"But aren't we taking our chairs and things, Mr. Olsen," Ellen asked.

"I'll come back for 'em later. Where's your boots, Letty?"

"Mr. Olsen, I don't think my father would want us to leave without taking our furniture with us."

"Look, my wife's going to take you to the Christmas celebration and you'll get presents from Santa Claus and everything. Only we gotta hurry, see?"

"Daddy's getting me a present," Letty said.

Robbie shouted, "I think we'd better wait here for Daddy."

"There'll be a Christmas tree," the sheriff said, "and hot cocoa to drink and peanut butter sandwiches. Robbie, you got brains, see if you can find Letty's mittens. I got her boots here."

Next Ellen spoke up: "We aren't supposed to go to the Christmas celebration, Mr. Olsen. My father told us it's just for the children who live in town."

"Well, that's the big surprise you pa's got for you. Santa Claus wants the three Reade kids to be special guests. Letty, stick your thumb in the hole that was meant for your thumb in this mitten."

"I want my daddy," Letty squealed. "I want my daddy to take me to see Santa Claus."

"She's scared because Daddy isn't here," Robbie said. "Aren't you scared 'cause Daddy isn't here, Letty?"

Sheriff Olsen grabbed hold of Letty. "How good

can you ride piggyback?" With that, he rushed her off to the car.

Going over the slippery road with the three children, the sheriff had to drive slowly and carefully back into town. Right away, when the sheriff honked, Johanna came running out of the house.

"Johanna, they haven't eaten yet. And could you please phone down to the Christmas committee and tell them that you're bringing three extra children so they will have time to get their gifts wrapped right."

Johanna opened the back door to the car, and the three Reade youngsters moved out toward the smile she gave them like they were three new-hatched chicks heading for the feel of something warm.

"Wow!" said Johanna. "Am I ever lucky! There's a whole big chocolate cake in the kitchen, and me worrying who was going to help to frost and eat it."

With the kids out of the car, the sheriff drove kind of crazy. Once he was past the courthouse and heading for the station, the traffic thinned out and there wasn't anybody's neck to worry about except his own.

The freight was in, and the sheriff drove straight up onto the platform. Lindahl, who was stationmaster, gave a yelp, but when he saw it was the sheriff, he yelled, "What's he look like?" and started running down the length of the train.

Sheriff Olsen headed east toward the engine, and found where somebody had once been crouching down in the snow on the embankment.

It was an open boxcar, and likely Reade had seen the sheriff already, but the sheriff called out Reade's name anyhow. Then he pulled himself up into the car.

It took half a minute for the sheriff to get used to the half light, but all that time Stephen Reade didn't move or try to get past him through the door. He just sat huddled up in his corner, pretending like he wasn't there.

Sheriff Olsen went over to him and put his hands under Reade's elbows and pulled him to his feet. Reade didn't say anything when the sheriff shoved him down off the boxcar into the snow. But when they were in the sheriff's car, the train gave a whistle and Reade said, in a whisper, "I was close to making it."

The sheriff drove around behind where the Ladies' Shakespeare Study Society had put a row of evergreens. He kept the heater going, and after a couple of minutes Stephen Reade stopped shaking some. The sheriff got out the vacuum bottle and poured coffee into its cap.

All of a sudden Reade gave a groan. "Let me out of here! For their sake, you've got to let me get away!" He started to rock back and forth, with his hands holding tight to his knees. "You've got to believe me! I'm no good for those kids! I've lost my nerve. I'm frightened. I'm frightened sick!"

For a long time the sheriff just sat next to Stephen Reade, wanting one minute to break the guy's neck for him, and the next minute to put his arm around him, and not knowing any of the time what was right to do.

After a couple of minutes he said, "A while back,

you claimed I didn't know what it was like to be scared. Well, sometimes I get scared, too. Take like this afternoon. This afternoon I got to dress up crazy and hand out presents to a whole roomful of kids. Last night I didn't sleep so good either, worrying about it."

Stephen Reade snorted.

"Well, it ain't easy like maybe you think," Sheriff John went on. "I have to get up on a platform, and all the kids'll be staring at me, and sometimes their folks come too."

"You certainly make it sound tragic."

"OK, if you don't figure it's so hard, you do it. I'll make a bargain with you. You be Santa Claus for me, and I'll find you a job. And while you're doing a good turn for both me and yourself, Ellen and Robbie and Letty will sure get a kick out of seeing their pa acting Santa Claus to all the kids in town."

For a long time Reade just sat staring through the windshield. Then he said, with his voice low and sober, "You couldn't find me a job. There isn't a man in the whole county who'd be half-wit enough to hire the loony that made hash out of Merske's farm. And you know it." Then he faced around to the sheriff. "But I'll play at being Santa Claus if you want me to. I've been owing you some sort of thanks for a couple of years."

Ten minutes later, the sheriff had Stephen Reade holed up in the washroom opposite his office. He pointed out where the outfit was hanging in the corner. "You better put the whiskers and cap on, too, while you

got a mirror," he said. "I'll keep watch outside."

Sheriff Olsen closed the washroom door and stepped back almost into his deputy's arms.

"What you got in there?" Mart Dahlberg said.

"Stephen Reade. He's going to be Santa Clause."

"You crazy or something?" Mart asked. "You've been Santa Claus for five years. What you want to go and give your part to that dope for?"

"Look, Mart, don't yell. Reade's feeling awful low, see? Getting evicted and not having a job or nothing. And I kinda figured handing out the presents to all the kids would maybe pep him up some."

"The committee won't let him."

"The committee won't know until it's too late," the sheriff explained. "Maybe I figured crazy, but I had to figure something. And, anyhow, he promised his kids a good surprise."

Mart gave a gentle pat on the sheriff's back. "Well," he said, "I can pray for you, but I don't figure it will help much."

Twenty minutes later, Sheriff Olsen poked his head into the kitchen behind the church's big recreation room.

Mrs. Bengtson looked around from washing cocoa cups. "The eating's done with, John," she said. "And they're singing carols while they wait for you."

Sheriff Olsen said, "Thanks." He motioned Stephen Reade to slip past through the kitchen to the door that opened out on the little stage. Then he moved himself, quiet and unnoticed, around to the back of the recreation room.

The piano was playing "Silent Night" and the place was jam-packed. The sheriff took off his hat and wiped his face. Then he sat down at the end of the bench that held Johanna and the three Reade kids. He smiled across the heads of the three kids at Johanna, and then he closed his hand over the hot paw that little Ellen had wriggled onto his knee.

Up on the stage the tree was a beautiful sight. It was nine feet tall, and the committee had decorated it with pretty balls, lights, and popcorn chains. Under the tree were the presents. The wrapping paper had all come from Merske's Dry Goods Store because this year Sam Merske was chairman of the committee and most of the presents had been bought at his store. Some of the paper was white and had green bells on it and some was red with white bells, and each bell had printed on it one of the letters of M E R S K E. And they were a beautiful sight, too. But sitting next to the presents, low under the tree, hunched up like a discouraged rabbit, was Santa Claus.

Sheriff Olsen flattened his hat out on his knee. Mart had been right. Wearing a beard on his chin and putting stuffing over his stomach weren't going to put pep into Stephen Reade. All they were going to do was spoil the show for the children and make Reade feel more miserable even than before! Then the music stopped and the sheriff folded his hat in two. Mart had said he would pray and maybe he wasn't forgetting to.

All of a sudden a little kid down front squealed, "Merry Christmas, Santa Claus!" And after that, the whole room was full of loving squeals and chirpings and calls of "Hi, Santa!"

Stephen Reade straightened up his shoulders a bit and then he reached out a hand for one of the packages. Sheriff Olsen began to feel some better. At least, Reade was remembering what he was up on the stage for, and maybe the kids wouldn't notice that Santa Claus didn't have his whole heart in the business.

Then a voice said, hoarse and angry, "Move over," and Sam Merske plunked himself down at the end of the bench.

Sheriff Olsen gave a low groan, and Merske said, "Surprised to see me, huh?"

"Kinda," the sheriff muttered.

"You got the nerve to be sitting here," Merske said. "Who you got up there behind those whiskers?"

Sheriff Olsen wet his lips and then he opened his mouth, figuring to say it was a friend. But Ellen Reade was quicker at opening hers. Ellen leaned over the sheriff's knees and lifted her face up, eager and excited.

"It's my father, Mr. Merske," she whispered. "Isn't he *wonderful*?" Then she gave a sigh like she was stuffed full of a good dinner, and turned back to stare at the stage again.

Sheriff Olsen stared at the stage too, but the tree and Santa Claus and the little boy who was getting his present were all blurred together because of the awful way the sheriff was feeling.

Sam Merske said, "So you put Stephen Reade up there in the whiskers and clothes and things that I supplied. Ain't that just beautiful?"

On the stage, a little girl was getting her package, and being a little girl, was remembering to say "Thank you."

Sam Merske said, "I'll get you for this. Putting a dead beat up there to hand out stuff that's wrapped with my paper and tied with my string! A no-good loafer that'll ruin the whole show! A no-good—"

His voice was getting louder, and the sheriff stuck his elbow hard into Sam Merske's ribs to make him shut up before the Reade kids could hear what he was saying.

But just shutting him up for now wasn't going to help. There were an awful lot of ways Merske could shame Stephen Reade in front of his children—like taking away the table and chairs that Ellen had counted on belonging to her family.

Sheriff Olsen tried to swallow, but his mouth was too dry. His throat was dry the same as his mouth. But his face and neck were so wet it would have taken a couple of bath towels to mop them.

It wasn't just a dumb thing the sheriff had gone and done; it was a plain crazy thing.

"Look, Sam," the sheriff whispered, "I gotta talk with you outside."

"Not with me," Merske said. "I'm sitting right here until I can lay my hands personal on that bum."

"Crazy" was what his deputy had called the sheriff's scheme. But Mart Dahlberg had been kind and gener-ous. "Wicked" was the word he ought to have used.

And then all of a sudden a little boy began to yowl.

"It's Johnny Pilshek," Ellen said. "He's mad 'cause Louie Horbetz got a cowboy hat and all he got was mittens."

Every year it happened like that. Two or maybe three or four kids would complain about their presents, and that was why the committee always hid half a dozen boxes of something such as crayons under the sheet to give them. But Stephen Reade didn't know about the extras, because the sheriff had forgotten to tell him.

Johnny Pilshek marched back up on the stage. He stuck out his lower lip and shoved the mittens at Santa Claus. "I don't want mittens," Johnny howled. "Mittens aren't a real present."

Santa Claus took the mittens and inspected them. "Most mittens aren't a real present," he said, "but these mittens are something special. They're made of interwoven, reprocessed wool, Johnny. That's what the label says. And we had to order them especially for you at the North Pole, Johnny! Everywhere, boys have been asking me to bring them this special kind of mitten, but we haven't been able to supply the demand."

"I've got mittens already," Johnny muttered. "I don't want no more."

Santa reached out and took one of Johnny's hands and inspected it careful as he had the mittens.

"Certainly you've got mittens already, Johnny. But they aren't like these. Do you know why we had these made for you, Johnny? We had these made for you because your hands are rather special. You've got to keep those fingers of yours supple, Johnny. A baseball player, when he's your age, gets his fingers stiff from the cold, and what happens? He winds up in the minor leagues, that's what happens."

He put the mittens back into Johnny's hand. "And we don't want you in anything except the major teams, Johnny."

"Gee," said Johnny. Then he turned around and walked down off the platform, flexing the fingers of his right hand, slow and thoughtful all the way.

Sheriff Olsen let out the breath he'd been holding; he could see now how Stephen Reade had made a living for his wife and kids out of going from door to door with magazines and hosiery and vacuum cleaners. The sheriff looked down at Ellen, and Ellen looked up at the sheriff and gave a big smile.

"He sure *is* wonderful!" the sheriff whispered to her.

And then a little girl sitting next to Johnny Pilshek stood up and asked, solemn and polite, if she could bring her present back too. She'd wrapped it up in the paper again, and she kept it hidden behind her until she was up on the stage.

"I think it's a mistake," she said in an unhappy kind of a whisper. "What I got wasn't meant for a girl."

Santa took the package. "We don't often make a mistake, April," he told her, "but let's see." He opened the package up on his knees.

"I don't mind it's being a muffler," April said, "but that one's meant for a boy. I know, because it's just like one they've got in Mr. Merske's store in the boy's section for 69 cents. And it's not one bit pretty, either."

Stephen Reade held up the heavy gray scarf. "You're right, April," he said. "This was made for a boy and it's not one bit pretty. All the same, we chose it for you. And here's the reason why. It was chosen especially to protect your voice."

"I don't care. I don't want to wear it."

"You're pretty, April, and someday you'll be even

103

prettier. But this is a fact. To get into the movies or on TV you've got to have a pretty face, but you've got to have something else too. You've got to have a pretty voice, one that's been properly protected by"—he turned over one corner of the scarf—"by 40 percent wool, 60 percent cotton, var-dyed."

He draped the thing over April's arm, and after a little bit, April began to stroke it.

"Should I wear it all the time, Santa?"

"No. Just when the temperature's below freezing, April. Have your mother check the thermometer every time you go out, and when it's below 32, then you wear it."

"Yes, sir—I mean, yes, thank you, Santa Claus."

Five minutes later, the lady who played the piano sat down again and started in on "Hark the Herald Angels Sing." On the stage Stephen Reade was standing up, singing, and motioning with his arms for everybody to join in. But the sheriff couldn't join in. He couldn't even open his mouth, let alone get any singing out.

Stephen Reade had done what the sheriff had asked him to, and he'd made a good job of it. And in return the sheriff had got Reade and his kids in a worse fix than ever.

The sheriff turned and looked at Sam Merske. He wasn't singing either—just scowling and muttering to himself.

The sheriff wet his lips. "Sam," he said.

Merske turned and glared. "So that was the gag," he said. "Pretty slick, pretty slick, arranging for him to give me a personal demonstration of his selling ability. Pretty slick."

"Huh?" said the sheriff, and when the song ended and the next one hadn't yet begun, he said, "Huh?" again.

"OK," said Merske, "you win this time. He gets the job."

"What do you mean?" the sheriff asked slow and careful. "You mean you're fixing to give Stephen Reade a job in your store?"

"With the competition I've got from the mail-orders, I'd give a shoplifter a job if he could sell like that guy can. He may not be a farmer, but he's a real salesman." Then he scratched at the top of his head and glared some more at the sheriff. "What gets me is that I never put you down for having either the brains or the brass to swing a deal like that. How'd you hit on it?"

Sheriff Olsen didn't answer. It would take an awful lot of talking to explain to Merske how sometimes things worked out fine even without any brains to help you. And, besides, the piano was getting started on "Jingle Bells," which was a tune the sheriff knew extra well.

Sheriff Olsen opened his mouth wide. He could tell from the way the folks in front turned around to frown at him that he was drowning them out. But he didn't care. There wasn't any better time than a week before Christmas, he figured, for bursting out loud and merry . . .

Mr. Sankey Celebrates Christmas

John Gillies

It's a long arm that stretches from guard duty near Sharpsburg, Maryland, during the Civil War to a Pennsylvania riverboat in 1875. It's almost eerie to witness such a graphic example of God's choreography.

The stocky, mustachioed man nervously paced the deck of a Delaware River steamer, unbuttoning his frock coat and regularly removing his derby to wipe his brow. He looked much older than his 35 years.

It was unseasonably warm for a Christmas Eve.

The man stared at the passing Pennsylvania shoreline, thinking of his family in Newcastle, some 300 miles to the west, whom he might not see this Christmas unless he made his train connection in Philadelphia. Christmas, 1875.

"Pardon me, sir."

"Aren't you Ira Sankey, the gospel singer?"

He smiled at the lady and her husband. He assumed the man was her husband. He thought he was gracious to acknowledge that he was, indeed, Ira D. Sankey.

"We've seen your pictures in the newspapers."

He had not wanted to be recognized—not today, not tonight. He was tired and fretful and warm. Fact of the matter was, he was angry and provoked with Mr. Moody.

"We thought you were still in England!" said the lady.

"We returned last week, madam," Mr. Sankey replied in his resonant baritone voice. And if Mr. Moody hadn't insisted on more conferences and meetings, he thought, he would have been home by now for Christmas with his family. Instead he was a prisoner on a river steamer.

"Mr. Sankey, would you sing for us? It is Christmas Eve. And we'd love to hear you."

Mr. Sankey said he would sing, and his presence was announced loudly across the deck. As the people gathered, he pondered what he might sing. He wished he had his portable pump organ, which had become an integral counterpart to his singing. But no matter. He would sing a Christmas carol or two, unaccompanied. Perhaps he would get the passengers to sing along with him.

He tried to shed his melancholy. He was a famous person, whether he liked it or not, and he was not normally shy about his gifts. He was known on two continents as the gospel singer, the song leader and soloist working with Dwight L. Moody, who was surely the greatest evangelist of the day. Perhaps God had intended it this way—for him to be in this place, on this boat, at this particular time.

"I thought I would sing a carol or two." Then, he added, "But somehow I feel I should sing another song."

"Sing one of your own songs!" shouted someone unseen. "Sing 'The Ninety-and-Nine!'" commanded another.

"No, thank you very much, but I now know what I must sing." He was smiling broadly now, feeling much better about himself and this situation, enjoying his congregation. "I shall sing a song by William Bradbury. And if you know it, as I'm sure many of you do, hum along with me."

Sankey began:

> Savior, like a shepherd, lead us,
> Much we need Thy tenderest care.
> In Thy pleasant pastures feed us
> For our use Thy folds prepare.
> Blessed Jesus, blessed Jesus,
> Thou has bought us, Thine we are.

He sang all three verses. There was uncommon silence and Ira Sankey felt it would be inappropriate to sing anything else. So he simply wished everyone a Merry Christmas and the people murmured a greeting in return. The silence returned and he was alone.

"Your name is Ira Sankey?"

"Yes." He recognized neither the voice nor the man.

The man came out of the shadows. He was about his own age, with a beard beginning to turn grey, and comfortably but not fastidiously dressed. Perhaps he was in sales, a traveling man.

"Were you ever in the Army, Mr. Sankey?"

"Yes, I was. I joined up in 1860."

"I wonder if you can remember back to 1862. Did you ever do guard duty, at night, in Maryland?"

"Yes, I did!" Sankey felt a stab of memory and excitement. "It might have been at Sharpsburg."

"I was in the Army, too. The Confederate Army. And I saw you that night."

Sankey looked at him warily.

"You were parading in your blue uniform. Had you in my sights, you standing there in the light of the full moon, which was right foolish of you, you know." The man paused. "Then you began to sing."

Amazingly, Sankey remembered.

"You sang the same song you sang tonight. 'Savior, Like a Shepherd Lead Us.' "

"I remember."

"My mother sang that song a lot but I never expected no soldier to be singing it at midnight, on guard duty. Especially a Union soldier." The man sighed. "Obviously, I didn't shoot you."

"And obviously, I am grateful," Sankey smiled.

"I always wondered who you were. Who it was I didn't kill that night, on account of his singing an old Sunday school song."

Sankey just shook his head.

"Frankly, up until tonight, the name of Ira Sankey wouldn't have meant much to me. Guess I don't read the paper like I should. I didn't know you'd turn out to be so famous!" The man smiled for the first time. "But I reckon I would have recognized the voice and the song anyplace."

Sankey reflected on what might have been.

"Do you think we could talk a mite?" asked the man.

"I think you owe it to me. Very little has gone right for me. Not before the war. Not during it. And not since."

Ira Sankey put an arm around his former enemy. They found a place in a quiet corner of the deck to sit and chat. Sankey's impatience and anger had passed. He no longer fretted that he might be delayed in seeing his family. Christmas would soon be here. It always came, but sometimes in the strangest ways.

The night was still warm but it seemed filled with brighter stars.

Sankey even thought he heard the sound of angels' voices—singing of course, and singing the Good News.

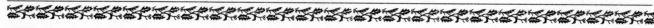

Stranger, Come Home

Pearl S. Buck

No one has ever bridged the vast yawning chasm between East and West more effectively than Nobel prize winner Pearl Buck. Having grown up as a child of two cultures, Buck was able to do what no previous American had ever done: speak from personal experience as well as from knowledge, from the heart as well as from the mind.

So when America fought in the Far East during World War II, the Korean War, and the Vietnam War, Buck was able to apply her insights and sensitivity to the broken lives and broken dreams that these wars left in their wakes.

Very late in her long and illustrious career, Mrs. Buck wrote "Stranger, Come Home," one of the most moving and haunting stories to come out of the Vietnam War.

"Merry Christmas, darling!"

David Alston heard his wife's voice from the edge of sleep and he opened his eyes. Nancy's pretty face, framed in dark curly hair, was bent over him; she was leaning on one elbow, half sitting up in the big double bed.

He yawned mightily and said, "Not you, Peanut! Kids, yes. One groans and takes it. But a man's wife? That's cruelty, especially on Christmas morning!"

Peanut was what he had called her in the days when they went to high school together, here in this little town in the Green Mountains of Vermont, he carrying her books and she skipping along somewhere near his elbow. He was tall and she was slight, dark to his blondness, gay to his gravity. He tried now to remember to call her Nancy in public and in front of the children, but she was Peanut when they were alone. He drew her down to kiss her. She yielded with a nice readiness, drawing back only when she became breathless.

"I couldn't sleep," she said.

"Why not?" he asked wryly. "We didn't get to bed until one in the morning. I thought I'd never get those pedal carts put together—one was bad enough, but three! I knew the boys had to have them this Christmas, but I didn't think Susan would want one, too."

"She wants whatever the boys have . . . David!"

"Yes? What now?"

"Do you think they'll see?"

"See what?"

"You know what I mean."

He sat up and put aside the covers. "Now, Peanut, you know we said we weren't going to worry. We said that from the very beginning—or as soon as we decided what to do about Susan. We said we'd take the chance."

He disappeared into the bathroom and she lay thinking, trying not to feel apprehensive. For this was a Christmas Day not like any other, and the house held a secret unlike any other—a child whose real identity must be hidden forever. Everyone was to believe that Susan was a little half-American waif from Vietnam, her mother a Vietnamese girl, her father a GI. No one was to know, not even if she did have the honey blonde hair, the amber eyes that all the Alstons had. Still, with her Asian face, it might be possible that no one would guess. Perhaps David's younger brother, Richard, didn't even know there had been a child. And yet . . . the child was named Susan; the name was a family name, David's mother's and grandmother's.

Nancy closed her eyes. So much had happened in the past year! Was it possible that only a year ago Sister Angelica's letter had come from the convent in Saigon, telling of the birth of the baby girl named Susan?

"Thu Van would never tell us the name of the father," Sister Angelica wrote. "Only when she was dead did we find his picture, wrapped in white silk. The address was on the back."

Had Thu Van killed herself? Sister Angelica, in her second letter, had said it was possible.

Nancy herself, upon reading the letter, had said so to David. "I think she did."

"Why?" he had demanded.

"Because—if she loved him and knew he was never coming back—"

Nancy was interrupted in her thoughts. The door burst open and her two small sons rushed into the room, still in their pajamas. They stopped at the sight of the half-empty bed. "Where's Daddy?"

"In the bathroom," she said.

They ran to the bathroom door.

"Daddy, it's not fair!" Jimmy shouted.

"You're not supposed to get up first on Christmas!" Ricky added.

David stuck his head out from behind the shower curtain. "Your mother woke me up—you'll have to speak to her!"

"Mommy—you're naughty!" The boys' faces were alive with mischief.

"I know I am," she confessed. "What shall we do with me?"

They paused to consider this, their eyes big. Two adorable little boys, she thought, straight blond hair, amber eyes, Alstons both. Ricky, the younger, had been named for Richard, who was safely home from Vietnam when Ricky was born.

Nancy remembered how silent Richard had been

in those days, how difficult, how torn by feelings he never divulged. She and David had been glad when, after months of indecision, he had suddenly decided to marry Miranda. Now, of course—Nancy broke off her thoughts and turned to the door.

"Come, Susan," she said.

The little girl, a year younger than Jimmy, a year older than Ricky, stood hesitating at the open door, her great eyes, exquisitely shaped, the corners lifted, wide and watchful. She came forward slowly, doubtfully. She was a grave child, her perfect little face seldom changing. Nancy put her arm about the slender figure in the pink pajamas.

"Merry Christmas," she said. "Merry Christmas to you and to Jimmy and to Ricky! Merry means happy. We'll all be happy today."

She kissed the little girl's cheek and went on. "Everybody get dressed—yes, yes, I know—" she held up a hand. The two boys, now jumping on the bed and starting a pillow fight, were beginning to protest. Nancy went on. "I know we don't usually get dressed first, but we're all awake, Daddy's nearly ready, and today we must be early because Uncle Richard and Aunt Miranda are coming. We can't be in pajamas when they arrive, can we?"

"Off the bed, boys," David ordered. "You heard your mother!"

The voice of authority, and they ran to obey. Only Susan stood motionless within the circle of Nancy's arm. How much did the child understand? She spoke French, but shyly, her voice very soft.

"*Et tu, aussi, ma chérie,*" Nancy said tenderly.

"Don't use French," David said quickly. "She shouldn't hear anything except English. She's ours now."

"Come with me, Susan," Nancy said. "I'll help you dress." She paused at the door, the child clinging to her hand.

"Will you light the tree, David? We shan't be long. I won't let the boys go downstairs first, because I want Susan to see the tree at the same time. I wonder if she's ever seen a Christmas tree?"

"Who knows?" David said.

"There's so much we don't know," Nancy said.

Downstairs, David lighted the tree, and, while he was waiting for the others, began thinking of all he did know.

* * * * *

Sister Angelica had written voluminous letters, but there was more behind and beyond those letters. David was 10 years older than Richard and, when their parents died in an airplane crash, he had tried to take his father's place.

Because of Richard, David had postponed his own marriage. Somehow he had managed to keep this house going, working at the bank and earning enough to eke out the small inheritance their parents had left them. When at last he had married Nancy it was to this home he had brought her. It was inconceivable that they live elsewhere than in this rambling white frame house with the green shutters, standing on a wide, shaded street, the elm trees today laden with Christmas snow. To such a house, American for 200 years, a little half-Asian child had come home. How strange the times!

David remembered how long and difficult the years before his marriage had been. College and then postgraduate work for his younger brother had taken all he could spare, but Nancy had waited for him in understanding patience. It was obvious that Richard was brilliant, and he wanted to be an international lawyer. After the long years of school and summer training jobs, Richard had been called for military service and sent to Vietnam. Now he had a post in the government in Washington, a beginning for a career that already promised success.

Richard and Miranda had waited, too, for he had come back not wanting to be married at once. Miranda's family had money, her father was a senator, and Richard, always proud, had maintained that he would not marry until he could give her a home and a place in a community where she could be happy. Finally, almost a year and a half ago, the marriage had taken place and it was to all appearances happy.

Then last Christmas the greeting card had come from Thu Van, written in French, addressed only by surname—"Monsieur Alston." David had taken it for granted that it was for himself until he read the card: "At this time of the blessed Noël, Richard, my beloved, I write to tell you I am still alive and always loving you. May the good God bless you, is the wish of my longing heart! I forget never. Your Thu Van."

David knew at once what it meant. Richard had loved a girl in Vietnam. This explained everything, his melancholy when he came home, his silence, his wish to postpone his marriage, everything that made him so different from the vigorous and articulate young man he had always been.

David showed the card to Nancy and on Christmas Day they were still discussing what to do. David had been inclined to send no answer. "Certainly I shall not give this card to Richard," he had said in firm decision this day a year ago. "Richard is just settled in a splendid job," he had told Nancy. "Think what this would do to him if it were known—if he knew what we know!"

Nancy, winding up a toy monkey for Ricky, had looked thoughtful. "I feel sorry for that girl," she said. "I do feel you should write to her and explain that you read the letter, thinking it was for you. You could tell her that your brother is happily married and that you do not think it kind or useful to disturb his life, especially since he is no longer with us but lives in another city. Be honest with her—say you aren't giving her card to him. Otherwise her heart will break when there's no answer from Richard."

In the end, David had followed Nancy's advice and had written Thu Van. An answer came, not from her but from Sister Angelica. It, too, was in French.

"Monsieur," Sister Angelica wrote. "Your esteemed letter has come too late. Thu Van died here in the convent on the afternoon of the day of Noël. She had been very sad after the departure of your brother, and since we love her as a former student we had begged her to come and spend the holiday with us. She brought to us her small daughter, Susan, born four years ago. This is your brother's child.

"When I saw the sadness of Thu Van, I inquired of its cause and she told me that your brother and she had a warm affair of the heart, but that he did not marry her. He does not know of the birth of this child. She preferred not to cause him grief by telling him. He left when she was three months pregnant.

"It is her noble nature not to wish to cause pain. Her position became difficult, however, since her family is a well-known one. She was no ordinary prostitute, but a young woman of dignity as well as great beauty who met your brother, then a young officer, in the home of a French friend. It seems they fell in love immediately and at once the situation became passionate.

"To continue, she spent Noël with us here at the convent, keeping the child beside her all day. After the little one was put to bed, it is said by some that she took one of those swift and subtle poisons that people of the East know so well how to use. Since she was Catholic, I doubt her capable of such sin. But perhaps! At any rate, the child's crying in the morning woke us early, and since it continued we went into the room and found the young mother lying on her pallet, dead.

"It remains now the question of what to do with the child. Is it possible the father would wish to claim her? Since he has a wife, it may be that they would accept this child, and bring her up as their own. She inherits her mother's beauty and something also from her father. Her hair is light in color, her eyes are also light. She is of superior intelligence, as are most of these mixed children, we find. Instruct me, if you please, Monsieur, and I am your obedient servant."

David had handed the letter to Nancy and she read it in silence. They had no chance to talk until that night when the children were in bed, and then they were too tired to talk, too exhausted within by the emotions that all day they had not been able to share in the presence of others. But in the night, Nancy had awakened him.

"David!"

"Yes?"

"I can't sleep."

He had reached for the light, but she had stopped him.

"David!"

"Yes, my love?"

"We must take Susan," Nancy said firmly. "We must take her for our own."

How well he remembered her clear soft voice coming out of the night, there beside him!

"She belongs to our family," Nancy had said.

"I suppose there are thousands of such children," he had said uncertainly. "They can't all be brought here. Perhaps she'd better stay there in the convent. We could send money."

"I'd never be able to sleep again, thinking of her," Nancy said.

Difficulties rose to David's mind. "She may look like Richard," he demurred. "One thing is clear in my mind, Nancy. I won't have Richard's life and career destroyed simply because of a half-Vietnamese child—even though she's his."

Nancy had removed herself from his arms abruptly when he finished. "I think of her as half American," she said clearly, "and therefore half ours. And her mother is dead. She killed herself because she loved your brother hopelessly. And he did love her in some fashion because he let her love him. There's an obligation. And the letter says that in Asia the child belongs to the father. The father is your brother."

The upshot of her determination was that they had begun the long process of adopting Susan, not as Richard's child but as a waif, the child of an anonymous American soldier in Vietnam who might have been any soldier but whose mother, a Vietnamese lady, now dead, had left her in a convent.

The agency social worker had been doubtful and reluctant. "We must first see if we can find a Catholic family for this child of a Catholic," she had said.

They had gone through the long ordeal of waiting until in the end it was proved there was no Catholic family who wanted the child, at least within the area of the agency, and reluctantly Susan was given to them. It had taken a year shorter by one week, and so one week ago Susan had arrived at the airport in New York, and they had gone to meet her, he and Nancy. Susan had descended from the plane, the stewardess holding her hand, looking lost and tearful. Nancy had opened her arms then and the little girl had gone straight into that haven.

"I've always wanted a daughter," Nancy had said through her tears.

* * * * *

The door opened softly at this moment and David saw Susan standing there. She had come downstairs alone. It was the first act of her own volition. Until now she had stayed where she was put, followed where she was led. Here she stood, transfixed at the sight of the glittering tree. Nancy had bought her a red velvet dress with a wide white collar and had put it on her this morning. Above it her great eyes shone luminous and lit from within, and her straight blonde hair hung to her shoulders. She came nearer to the tree, softly on tiptoe, and then gazed at it, her finger on her lip.

"*Jolie,*" she whispered. "*Très, très jolie!*"

He watched her in fascination, surely the loveliest child ever born. He felt a foolish dart of jealousy that Richard was the father.

"Pretty," he said gently, "very, very pretty."

She turned her grave eyes to his face. "Pret-ty," she echoed. She had not allowed him to take her hand or lift her to his knee, clinging always to Nancy, but now when he held her little left hand she did not withdraw it. They were standing thus, side by side, when Nancy came flying down the stairs.

"Susan!" she called. "Oh, Susan!"

"She is here with me," he said.

Nancy came in breathless. "She came downstairs alone, David! I was helping Ricky. They're in such a hurry they can't get their shoes tied. So she simply came down alone!"

"I know," he said. "She stood there in the doorway. Then she came in. Look—she lets me hold her hand."

"Oh, the darling!" Nancy cried softly, and sat down in a chair opposite the tree. "It's more beautiful than ever, because it's a special Christmas."

At this, Susan withdrew her hand gently and tiptoed to Nancy's side. Then, pointing her forefinger at the tree, she whispered.

"Jolie—pretty?"

"Yes, dear." She lifted the little girl to her lap. "Oh, David, what if they see and *want* her?"

He shook his head, unbelieving, and then they heard the two boys thundering down the stairs to join them.

They all joined hands then and stood around the tree. David led them in singing "Tannenbaum, O Tannenbaum," and he saw Susan softly moving her lips but uttering not a sound. She's doing her best, he thought, her very best to be one of us, bless her.

After that the day burst into its usual happy turmoil, the boys shouting and exulting, asking questions, demanding help.

"Dad, how does this work?"

"Mom, show me how to do this puzzle, please."

And throughout, Susan sat on a small needlepoint stool, her gifts piled about her, opening them gravely one by one, examining each, and putting each in its place in a neat pile on the floor beside her. Ah, but the doll, of course! She had thought it part of the tree, it seemed, for last night they had set it on a branch near the top, securing it with a pink ribbon. Now Nancy cut the ribbon and lifted the doll down, a girl doll, small enough to hold comfortably. She put it in Susan's arms and the child received the gift as a treasure not to be believed.

"C'est pour moi?" she asked under her breath.

"Yes, darling, for you," Nancy said.

Looking at Susan's face, David smiled. "She has what she really wants," he said.

But Susan heard nothing. In the midst of the boys' shouts and laughter, in the midst of the exchange of gifts between the two adults, she sat absorbed, undressing the doll, examining the rubber-skinned body carefully, then dressing it again.

David and Nancy finished opening their gifts and were exchanging a kiss when a man's voice interrupted them.

"A merry Christmas, I'd say—if you can believe what you see!"

They looked up. In the doorway stood Richard and Miranda: snowflakes dotted their shoulders and clung in Miranda's red hair.

"It's snowing again," Miranda said. "We'll have

to start home early. But merry Christmas, meanwhile!"

David hurried to greet them and in the hall he helped Miranda with her coat while Richard hung his in the closet. David wanted to be in the room with Nancy when they saw Susan. There might be instant recognition! Nancy was standing in the doorway now. Don't try to hide the child, he thought. It's no use. We must be ready for whatever happens.

"Come into the kitchen," Nancy was saying. "I must put the turkey into the oven. It's a monster—the biggest we've ever had . . . a sort of celebration for our little Susan. It's a special Christmas in this house. I was just saying so. . . ."

She was shepherding Richard and Miranda toward the kitchen, an arm about each, and making talk as she went. "Come on, David, you have to help. I can't lift the bird."

So they were in the kitchen and there was a moment's respite—no, only a delay, and that was no use. Richard and Miranda stood smiling, watching, and Nancy looked away. They were a beautiful pair, she thought, Richard so blond and Miranda a red-haired angel.

They might make good parents for a child! Was David right in not telling them, in not leaving the decision to them? Has any person the right to make a decision for another, even his brother? In her place, were she Miranda, were she Richard, she would say no, let me decide for myself. But she was neither, and Richard was devoted to his career, a dedicated man, a single-minded man, who, if his ambitions were thwarted, would be destroyed. David had pointed that out to her again and again.

"If it were I," David had said, "I'd want to know. But then I'm not a single-minded man. Nor do I want a career in politics. There's nothing I couldn't leave, except my family. I'm a lawyer, yes, but a small-town lawyer. I can do a dozen other things—real estate, for example. Sure, I love my home, and it would hurt me to leave—but then I wouldn't leave. I'd just say to the neighbors, yes, I was a kid in Vietnam once upon a time. Nancy's my wife and she wants the child!"

David had taken Nancy's hand. "But Miranda wouldn't want the child, Nancy—you know that. She'd care about what people said. She and Richard would both be broken up. I know my own brother, as fine a fellow as ever lived, but—well. I know him. He's on his way up, and I can't take the responsibility of blocking that upward way. People are sticky about a man's past, if he's dreaming of a Washington career. I know there's no limit to Richard's dreams, and I know he's the caliber the nation needs."

Nancy had listened to this, had allowed herself to be convinced. Now she was unconvinced again. Oh, let the day take its course! If the child were recognized, then let it be so. If not—oh pray God, it's not!

"Come and see the children," she said brightly when the turkey was in. She led the way bravely, and David stepped ahead to her side.

"Susan is engrossed with her doll," he said. "Don't mind if she makes no response just now. She's a single-minded little soul."

Susan did not look up when the two couples came in. She was undressing her doll again, folding each small garment carefully as she took it off. The boys jumped to their feet.

"Uncle Richard—"

"Aunt Miranda—"

Miranda fended off Ricky, laughing. "Careful, Ricky, I've put on my best dress for you—"

Richard said, "Hi there, Jimmy," and sidestepped the violent embrace.

"Susan," Nancy called. "Come here, dear. This is Aunt Miranda."

Nancy went to the little girl, put the now naked doll into her arms, and led her forward.

"Aunt Miranda," she repeated distinctly. "And Uncle Richard."

Nancy glanced at David as she spoke and caught his solemn gaze. Now was the moment.

"What a pretty child," Miranda said. "How do you do, Susan?" She leaned and touched her lips to Susan's cheek.

Ricky interrupted. "Did you bring us presents, Aunt Miranda?"

"Oh, Ricky," Nancy said. "For shame!"

"For shame," Jimmy echoed. "But you always do, don't you, Uncle Richard?"

"Of course," the uncle said. "Only this time it's a present so big I have to have help. It's for both of you."

"I'll help!" Jimmy shouted.

"Me too," Ricky cried.

"Richard," Miranda said. "You haven't spoken to Susan!"

He had turned to the door but now he looked over his shoulder, the boys clinging to his legs.

"Hi there, Susan," he said. "All right, fellows, come on and help."

He went out to the car, David and the boys following, and Miranda sat down and smoothed her short skirt.

"We spent the night in Boston," she told Nancy. "Richard wanted to push through in one day, but I can't take such a long day, especially with the next day Christmas, which is always a little tiring with children, I find. You really must come to us next year, Nancy. You'd enjoy Washington."

"The children are used to being here at Christmas," Nancy said gently. "But it's sweet of you to think of us. And we'll understand if it becomes too difficult for you to get away."

She was watching Miranda's stone-gray eyes. No, Miranda never glanced at Susan. The little girl had gone back to her chair and was dressing the doll again. Her bright hair fell straightly on each side of her face, hiding it in shadow. But Miranda was looking out of the window. The snow was falling fast.

Miranda stirred in her chair. "We must start back early," she said. "Else we'll never make Boston tonight. We reserved the hotel room."

"Vermont keeps her roads open very well," Nancy said. Strange how quickly she and Miranda fell out of something to talk about! She was glad when the boys came back again, followed by the two men, carrying a huge box.

"Look!" Ricky shouted. "A train!"

"An electric train," Jimmy corrected.

"Wonderful!" Nancy breathed. "It'll take the rest of the day to put it up."

"Where?" David asked, after a quick look at Nancy. Nothing had happened, he realized. So far so good!

"How about the playroom downstairs?" Nancy suggested.

"Oh, no," Ricky protested. "We want it here by the tree."

"Just for today," David said. "We'll move it tomorrow."

"Not too difficult after we have the thing assembled," Richard said.

Richard never looked at Susan, now buttoning the doll's dress. She has nimble fingers, Nancy thought; Susan did everything with a careful perfection. Oh, really, she could not spare this child!

The snow fell softly through the long morning until noon, and then stopped. The sun slanted its way through the clouds and dispelled them. The scent of roasting turkey drifted through the house as the two women set the table with Nancy's best silver and china, and decorated it with sprigs of holly.

"Party favors, as usual, for the children," Nancy said, "but when the crackers pop I hope Susan won't be frightened."

"She hasn't left off playing with that doll all morning," Miranda said. "I wish I'd had time to get the child a present, Nancy, but we didn't get your letter saying she was here until Christmas Eve and you know what it's like to shop then."

"She doesn't miss it," Nancy said.

"A queer-looking little thing, with that Asian face and that light hair."

"We think she's beautiful," Nancy said.

"She doesn't talk much, does she?"

"Of course, she does—perfect French and already beginning in English."

"Was she homesick?"

"No. She was told she was coming home—to us."

"What about her mother?"

"She's dead."

"Are there a lot of these children?"

"Many, we're told."

"So that's what our men are so busy about abroad!"

"Not all of them, I'm sure. . . . Does Richard like his salad with the turkey?"

"He doesn't like salad, period. Remember?"

"Ah, I'd forgotten. . . . Now everything is ready, I think. I love Christmas dinner."

"I'm sorry that you can't have it at night—"

"Oh, midafternoon is the only time if there're children. They get too tired playing all day and then if they have a big dinner. . . ."

Idle talk, she thought, but somehow there was never much else to talk about with Miranda. But perhaps she was to blame, for Miranda had been a writer for a woman's page before she was married, and she, Nancy, had never been anything but David's wife. Did she feel a slight inferiority to this smart woman from Washington? No, she did not!

"Dinner!" she called into the living room. "The turkey can't wait."

They all came out then to the dining room, the boys reluctant to leave their toys.

"We have the track assembled and the engine working," David reported. He lifted Susan into her chair. "And this afternoon we'll get the train moving. You must have spent a pretty penny, Richard."

"It was fun," Richard said briefly.

"A beautiful set," David said.

He glanced at Nancy and shook his head slightly. Nothing, he conveyed to her inquiring eyes—nothing at all. He didn't look at the child.

"Everyone sit down," David said. "And no one may talk while I carve the bird. It takes concentration and skill! And loving care."

"What's loving care, Daddy?" Ricky inquired.

"It means to go slow and take it as it comes,"

David said. He sharpened the carving knife meticulously and then all eyes were on him as the first slice was carved, brown-skinned on top and white inside.

All eyes, that is, except Miranda's. She was gazing at Susan, who sat at Nancy's side.

"I declare," Miranda said suddenly. "That child looks enough like the boys to be their sister—the same blond hair, the same color eyes!"

Richard looked at Susan. "You're right," he said. He laughed. "And don't look at me, please, Miranda! There were thousands of American boys over there and a lot of them had light hair and eyes."

Miranda laughed. "Thank God for that!"

"Thank God, anyway," David said, gravely. Again his eyes met Nancy's at the end of the table. Steady, he was saying to her, steady now.

"Here's your plate, Miranda," he said. "You're the first to be served."

Miranda took her plate, forgetting the child, and neither she nor Richard saw what Susan did, nor heard what she said. Under Miranda's half-idle stare Susan had put out her hand to Nancy.

"*Merci*, Mama," she whispered.

"I'm here, Susan," Nancy said. Putting out her own hand she clasped the small searching one. "Mama's here."

"Tell Me a Story of Christmas"

Bill Vaughan

How strange that clarity of vision blurs rather than sharpens with the passing of the years. In this brief but poignant story, a little girl gradually corrects her father's inner vision: without a moment's hesitation, she steers a straight course through mountains of pyrite to the mother lode itself.

Bill Vaughan, of the (Kansas City) Star, *was known as one of America's premier columnists and humorists. But of all his prodigious output, it is this short piece that* Star *readers ask for year after year. According to* Star *reporter Mike Henderson, if the* Star *were ever to get through a Christmas season without reprinting it, readers would boycott the paper!*

Tell me a story of Christmas," she said. The television mumbled faint inanities in the next room. From a few houses down the block came the sound of car doors slamming and guests being greeted with large cordiality.

Her father thought awhile. His mind went back over the interminable parade of Christmas books he had read at the bedside of his children.

"Well," he started, tentatively, "once upon a time, it was the week before Christmas, all little elves at the North Pole were sad . . ."

"I'm tired of elves," she whispered. And he could tell she was tired, maybe almost as weary as he was himself after the last few feverish days.

"OK," he said. "There was once, in a city not very far from here, the cutest wriggly little puppy you ever saw. The snow was falling, and this little puppy didn't have a home. As he walked along the streets, he saw a house that looked quite a bit like our house. And at the window . . ."

"Was a little girl who looked quite a bit like me," she said with a sigh. "I'm tired of puppies. I love Pinky, of course. I mean story puppies."

"OK," he said. "No puppies. This narrows the field."

"What?"

"Nothing. I'll think of something. Oh, sure. There was a forest, way up in the North, farther even

119

than where Uncle Ed lives. And all the trees were talking about how each one was going to be the grandest Christmas tree of all. One said, 'I'm going to be a Christmas tree, too.' And all the trees laughed and laughed and said, 'A Christmas tree? You? Who would want you?'"

"No trees, Daddy," she said. "We have a tree at school and at Sunday school and at the supermarket and downstairs and a little one in my room. I am very tired of trees."

"You are very spoiled," he said.

"Hmmm," she replied. "Tell me a Christmas story."

"Let's see. All the reindeer up at the North Pole were looking forward to pulling Santa's sleigh. All but one, and he felt sad because . . ." He began with a jolly ring in his voice but quickly realized that this wasn't going to work either. His daughter didn't say anything; she just looked at him reproachfully. "Tired of reindeer, too?" he asked. "Frankly, so am I. How about Christmas on the farm when I was a little boy? Would you like to hear about how it was in the olden days, when my grandfather would heat up bricks and put them in the sleigh and we'd all go for a ride?"

"Yes, Daddy," she said, obediently. "But not right now. Not tonight."

He was silent, thinking. His repertoire, he was afraid, was exhausted. She was quiet, too. *Maybe,* he thought, *I'm home free. Maybe she has gone to sleep.*

"Daddy," she murmured. "Tell me a story of

Christmas." Then it was as though he could read the words, so firmly were they in his memory. Still holding her hand, he leaned back:

"And it came to pass in those days, that there went out a decree from Caesar Augustus, that all the world should be taxed . . ."

Her hand tightened a bit in his, and he told her a story of Christmas.

The Bells of Christmas Eve

Joe L. Wheeler

Two women sat at the feet of Christ: Mary and Martha. There is something in most of us that identifies with the beautiful Mary—so effusive, appreciative, responsive, and filled with the joy of life!

But there was the second sister, not nearly so flamboyant, whose love manifested itself not in mere rhetoric but in service. It is the Marthas among us who carry on their shoulders the burdens of the world. It is the Marthas who nurture and sustain the eagles who fly so perilously close to the sun.

But Marthas have their dreams, too.

W hen will the bells ring?"

"Midnight, Miss Louisa . . . midnight."

"Thank you, Jacques. I'll . . . I'll be waiting. Don't forget the carriage."

"I won't, Miss Louisa."

She turned and walked to the hotel window, leaned against the sill, and waited. Waited, as was her custom, for the dying of the day. She sighed with a faint feeling of loss, for the sudden disappearance of the silver path to the sun that had so recently spanned the deep blue Mediterranean sea and sky.

Losing all track of time, her soul's lens recorded on archival film every detail as the master scene painter of the universe splashed all the colors and hues on His palette across the gilding sky. At the peak of intensity, she felt like a child again, watching that last heart-stopping explosion of fireworks that transforms mundane evening darkness into a twilight of the gods.

Then, as suddenly as it had come, it was over—and the curtain of night was drawn down to the darkening sea.

It was only then that the icy blade of loneliness slashed across her heart . . . and time ceased to be.

* * * * *

How much time passed before awareness returned, she never knew, for the breakers of awareness came in soft and slow, seemingly in unison with those breaking on the French Riviera shore outside the window.

Fully awakened at last, she slipped into her heavy coat, stepped outside, and walked across lawn and sand to her favorite rocky shelf. After snuggling down into a natural hollow out of the path of the winter wind, she spread her coat over her legs and wrapped a small blanket around her shoulders.

The tide was ebbing now, and with its departure she again realized how terribly lonely were the shores of her inner world . . . If only *he* were here to hold her, to commune with her, to fill that void in her life that only he could fill, achieve that sense of completeness that only he could induce.

Scenes from the past summer flashed on the screens of her mind: his arrival in a huge carriage at the Pension Victoria; her almost instant recognition of his weakened health; his stories detailing his involvement in the ill-fated Polish revolt against Russian tyranny, his capture and incarceration in a damp airless dungeon, and his eventual release.

Fresh from her service as a nurse in Washington during the recent American Civil War, she noted the same battle symptoms that marked tens of thousands of her own countrymen: the tell-tale signs of a weakened constitution, and the lingering evidence of recent illness and almost unendurable stress and pain. Instinctively, she steered the newcomer over to a table near the largest porcelain stove. That simple act of kindness supplied the spark that short-circuited the stuffy formalities of the day: one moment they were complete strangers; a moment later they were friends.

She was a 33-year-old June to his 21-year-old April. But hers was a young-at-heart 33, and his a maturity far beyond his years, forged by the crucible of war and imprisonment. But it was his seared, but cheerful still, spirit that won her heart. In spite of his recent residence in hell, this bruised and tattered lark was a living embodiment of the poetical portrayal of two men looking out through selfsame bars, one seeing walls, the other stars. Ladislas Wisniewiski saw the stars.

Used to the cold formality and austerity of New England, she was totally unprepared for warm-hearted Ladislas, who smashed through conventions and formalities as though they were so much kindling, a Mozart minuet stormed by a Liszt rhapsody.

In truth, Louisa had been the object of many a lovesick swain through the years, but none had been able to break through her self-imposed barriers of reserve and indifference; prior to Ladislas, not one had been able to raise her temperature so much as one degree.

The days and evenings that followed were full of adventures, large and small. He taught her French and she taught him English; he regaled her with the culture, history, and lore of the alpine country of Switzerland and France, and she introduced him to the New World of America; they rowed almost daily on beautiful Lake Geneva, framed by the snowcapped Alps; they explored the grounds of the chateau and area sights of interest such as the nearby Castle of Chillon, which Byron had immortalized; they took frequent tramps along the mountain sides, pausing often to drink in the stunning deep blue sheet of water spread out below them, the verdant hills around them, and the sawtooth mountains above them, cutting notches in the sky.

And woven into the fabric of that never-to-be-forgotten summer of '65 was talk—talk when talk added color, silence when talk was superfluous. Their talk recognized no barriers, no constraints. The subject was life, life with all its complexities, inequities, and unanswered questions. In the evenings, Ladislas would perform in the parlor (he was an accomplished professional musician), and Louisa would join the others and listen. Deep, deep within her, seas long

dead would be stirred into tempests by Ladislas's fomenting fingers.

He was good for her—far better than she knew, for Louisa was (and always had been) a caregiver, a Martha, one who sublimated her own dreams and desires so others could fulfill theirs. All her life, others had always come first. She had grown up early, realizing while yet a child that it was her beloved mother who bore the full weight of the family's financial problems, for her father—bless him!—seemingly dwelt in another world. Like Dickens' immortal Micawber, he blithely assumed that something would always "turn up" to enable the family to muddle through. Certainly, God would provide. Somehow, some way, God always did, but in the process her mother, Abba, grew old before her time.

Louisa had early recognized that she, by nature and temperament, was born to be an extension of her mother. She had sometimes resisted and resented this burden, but not for long, for hers was a sunny disposition; duty was not an ugly Puritan word but something you shouldered with a song in your heart.

Rummaging around in her mind, Louisa took off a dusty cobwebby shelf a Christmas reel of her childhood: images of that bitterly cold New England winter flooded the walls of memory. They were down to their last few sticks of wood, and the winter wind howled around the snow-flocked house, icy fingers reaching in through every crack and crevice and chink. Besides the three sisters, a newborn was now at risk when the firewood was gone. "God will provide," was her father's rejoinder to his wife's worried importuning. "God will provide as He always has."

Just then, there was a knock on the door. A neighbor had braved the banshee winds to bring over a load of wood, unable to escape the conviction that the family needed firewood. "Needed firewood?" Abba's face resembled a rainbow on a golden morning.

Later that memorable evening, Father had disappeared for some time. When he returned, stomping his half-frozen feet on the fireside hearth to restore circulation, he jubilantly announced that another neighbor, with a sick baby in a near-freezing house, had asked for help—how providential that the Lord had sent his family wood. Abba's face grew coldly pale: "You . . . you didn't . . . certainly, you *didn't!*" But she knew even before he answered that he had. How *could* he? *They* had a baby too! This was just more than flesh and blood could bear.

But before her pent-up wrath could erupt there was another knock on the door—and another load of wood waited outside. "I told you that we would not suffer," was her father's trusting response. Abba and her girls just looked at each other, absolutely mute.

* * * * *

Louisa stirred, aware of a change in the tide: it was beginning to return. A dream-like full moon had risen, and the breakers were now luminous with a ghostly beauty. The wind had died down at last.

Truant-like, before she knew they had slipped away, her thoughts returned to that golden summer in Vevey. How lonely she had been. At first, the mere idea of seeing Europe had entranced her; all she had to do was care for a family friend's invalid daughter: be a companion. But the girl was so insensitive to the beauty and history Louisa revelled in that her *joie de vivre* had begun to fade.

And then came Ladislas.

He filled a long-aching void in her life, for, growing up, she had been so tall, coltish, and tomboyish that romance could be found only in storybooks and in dreams. Her sisters were the soft, the feminine, the lovely ones.

Then, when she had grown up, this ugly-duckling self-image refused to go away, in spite of the refutation in her mirror and in the eyes of men. As a result, she remained shy and unsure of herself—and certainly, so far, success in her chosen career was mighty slow in coming.

Ladislas had unlocked an inner Louisa that even she had never seen before. Free for the first time in her life to be young without heavy responsibilities and worries, her day-by-day interactions with Ladislas brought new gentleness and vivacity to her face, and his open adoration, stars to her eyes. The older travelers staying at the pension watched the couple, subconsciously envying their youth and happiness. In the evening, in the flickering candlelight, Louisa's face was graced by that inner radiance that comes but once in a woman's life: from the full knowledge that she is loved and adored by the man she perceives to be her world.

She borrowed not from the future but accepted each day, each hour, each minute, as a gift from God. The realities of life were swept aside to dissipate in the mists of the mountains as they lived each moment with the intensity of those who live on the slopes of a volcano or on an earthquake fault. Time enough for harsh realities later, when the cherubims of circumstance barred them from Eden with their flaming swords.

But like all Shan-gri-las, this one too had to end. As the cool autumn winds swept down from Mont Blanc, Louisa's invalid charge decided it was time to move to a warmer climate—southern France would be ideal.

Louisa tearfully packed her trunks. It was no longer possible to pretend that this idyllic island in time would be their home. The age differential, Ladislas's lack of livelihood prospects and his weakened health, their cultural differences, Louisa's commitments to her family as well as her own career uncertainties—and, of course, the slight tincture of the maternal in her love for him—all added up to a gradually growing conviction that it would never be. Even as they rowed together, it was her sister, May, whom she envisioned opposite Ladislas down through the years; her age equating with his, her love of music and art responding to his, her infectious love of life feeding upon his boyish blandishments, impulsiveness, and warm and tender heart.

But none of this took away from the bittersweet parting. Masking his intense feeling, he kissed her hand in the European manner. As she watched his waving scarf recede into a blur down the train tracks, her eyes filled with tears.

For what right had she to dream of marriage? She who had vowed to shore up her mother's failing strength, assisting her in every way possible; and then, when that beloved caregiver could no longer function very well, quietly and cheerfully taking her place.

Then, too, Louisa vaguely realized that she was out of step with most of the women of her age, in that marriage, children, and domesticity was really not her, all in all. For she had career dreams of her own, and had little inclination to turn over her life to a man, becoming old before her time by repeated pregnancies and brutally heavy housework.

But even that could not check the tears running down her cheeks . . . for love is not governed by the mind.

* * * * *

She pulled out her watch and, by the light of the climbing moon, discovered it was almost 11. Just before midnight, she planned to take a carriage to the ancient cathedral and see the nativity scene everyone had been talking about. She hungered to hear the choir and pipe organ celebrate the birth of Jesus 18 and a half centuries ago.

In her pocket was a letter from home (worn and tattered from many readings) that her fingers touched in the darkness. She had no need to reread it for she knew it by heart: Father's lecture tours were not doing very well; Anna had just given birth to her second son (how good John was to her!); Mother continued to weaken, her gradual buckling to the resistless juggernaut of the years becoming ever more apparent to the writer of the letter, May; and as for May—how much she needed a chance to flower, to become a real artist: she must be given the opportunity to experience Europe, too.

And never far from mind was Beth—little Beth with her endearing ways, whose untimely death seven years before had left an aching void that time would never fill or completely heal. What a *dear* family she had! And how they loved each other! Wouldn't it be wonderful if she could use her writing talents to somehow recapture those magical childhood years, so permeated with sunlight and shadows, laughter and tears.

But every story, especially a story of four girls, has to have a hero, too. Perhaps—the image of a dark-haired Polish musician, forever teasing, laughing, and cajoling . . . She could no more resist him than she could the incoming tide now lapping at her feet. Brother, sweetheart, and friend. But "Ladislas" would never do. Um-m . . . how about "Lawrence" . . . but she'd call him "Laurie."

She sank into a reverie outside the stream of time. She had no way of foreseeing the future: of knowing that four months later, "Laurie" would be waiting for her at the train station, and that for two wonderful weeks he, she, and Paris in the spring would coalesce in memories that would never die. Nor could she

know that three years later, her book, the first half of the story, would be published, and a year after that, the second-half sequel would be snapped up by a constantly growing audience. The book would become the most beloved story ever written about an American girl. For, in spite of all her efforts to show off her sisters, offsetting their portraits with unvarnished depictions of her own frailties, mistakes, and weaknesses, she would fail in her purpose—for it would be Jo with whom generations of readers would fall in love.

And who among us could ever read that unforgettable passage, set in the eternally flowering gardens of Vevey, wherein Amy, still mourning the recent death of her sister Beth, looks up . . . and sees him standing there:

> "Dropping everything, she ran to him, exclaiming, in a tone of unmistakable love and longing, 'Oh, Laurie, Laurie, I knew you'd come to me!' "

Yes, who among us could ever read that without sensing that the words were really Jo's, that the broken heart was really Jo's, and that the longing for a love that would forever remain imprisoned in the bud of might-have-been, never blossoming into the rose of marriage, was Jo's. Who among us can read that heart-broken call without tears?

* * * * *

"Miss Louisa? . . . uh, Miss Alcott?"

"Uh . . . I'm sorry, Jacques, I guess I . . . I must have dozed off. What is it?"

"You asked me to have the carriage ready at 15 minutes before midnight."

"Oh, yes! Thank you—just give me a minute."

Soon Louisa was settled within the carriage. The horses snorted in the cold night air, and the wheels complained as they chattered and clattered over cobblestone streets. She looked out her window and took in the festive crowd and air of expectancy that hovered over the city. She realized that she regretted nothing—even if she had the opportunity to live her life over again she would change not one line. Joy and pain, hand-in-hand—without both she would have but a one-dimensional ditty or dirge; with both, a multifaceted symphony of life.

She could ask for no more.

Then she heard them, faint at first, soon gathering power as they were joined by other bells across the city. The crescendo continued until the ringing and the clanging swallowed up every other sound on earth.

It was Christmas . . . Christ was born in a manger.

* * * * *

Written December 1990. I am deeply indebted to Cornelia Meigs, for without her moving Invincible Louisa, *with its invaluable biographical material and discussion of the evolution of* Little Women, *this story would never have been. And I must not forget my American literature class at Columbia Union College—it was the lecture I wrote for them that inspired this story.*